IT'S THE RIGHT TIME FOR LOVE

Mistletoe, Jingle Bells, and Second
Chances Collection

By

Lana Newman Kruse

Martha ~
my lovely
sister-in-Christ.
friend and
Blessings and love!
Lana
Eph. 2:10
October 28, 2017

ISBN:1548683574
ISBN-13:9781548683573

Dedication

I happily dedicate this book to my fearless critiquers Anne Greene, Linda Baten Johnson, and Jim Yarbrough who were instrumental in getting this book ready for you, the reader. They read with care, respect, wisdom, and humor.

To my husband David who exhibited extreme patience and rose to every occasion to repair the countless technical glitches that occurred! To my daughter Kimberly, the forever cheerleader, who encouraged me to write, and then kept up the enthusiasm along with her husband Norm, my son Kyle, and his wife Amanda. And, to my amazing baby grands Abby, Luke, Mary-Claire, Anna, David, and Joshua whose eagerness and faith in their Mimi kept me going!

To all my friends and extended family who prayed, listened, and rallied round me when I needed it most!

And, most importantly, to my Lord and Savior Jesus Christ, my focus, my life, and the Author of everything good, who is able to accomplish more than I could ask or think.

Ephesians 3:20 Now all glory to God, who is able, through His mighty power at work within us, to accomplish infinitely more than we could ask or think. NLT

IT'S THE RIGHT TIME FOR LOVE

Chapter 1

Angela Elizabeth Cooper shook her fist in the air—Scarlet O'Hara style. Today her life would begin, even on this snowy, chilled-to-your-garters Valentine's Day, when all the calendars screamed LOVE. All calendars except hers. She would join the human race again, to which most of her family and friends belonged. She had to feel something, anything. This gripping numbness was worse than grief.

She'd stomp through her gift for melancholy and stab depression with bouts of hilarious laughter and silliness. She had a sense the world existed in warmth and coziness and vowed to find that toasty, cozy part.

"Ansey, you said you'd never leave me, but you did! You even promised." She jerked off her house shoe and hurled the red slipper at his framed photograph smiling at her from the antique desk. The picture crashed to the living room floor in sprays of glass that swept assorted what-nots with it.

"Grams, what was that?" Piper's voice thundered from upstairs.

Angie sank into her favorite French chair.

Footsteps padded on the carpeted stairs and grew louder as Piper whipped through the arched doorway into the living room. "Grams!" Piper's voice cracked, her long chestnut brown hair bouncing. "Grams! Are you all right?"

Angie smiled, enclosed in the warmth of Piper's hug. "Yes, honey, I'm fine." She grimaced and straightened. She kissed Piper's rosy cheek and gave her a gentle push to release her from their embrace. "Just knocked over Granddad's picture. Clumsy me."

Fine as she *could* be. Two long years since Ansey died. Blood rushed to her head in palpitating rhythm, and pain stabbed her temples.

"Grams, you sit tight, and I'll clean up this mess." In a split second Piper returned with broom and dust pan in hand.

"Oh, honey. I'll do that." Angie reached for the broom.

Piper twisted away. She smiled, jabbered, and swept.

Piper's muttering was akin to the seven dwarfs' *whistling while they worked*...only her granddaughter bubbled with words instead. All about school, getting married this Christmas Eve, and about how much she loved Granddad.

How much joy Piper brought into her life.

Piper Elizabeth Lacey, her firstborn grandchild, a delight from the day she was born.

"Honey, what am I gonna do when you leave? Having you here has been a wonderful treat these past two years."

"You'll do great, like always." Piper's face lit up like a sunbeam escaping through clouds on a rainy day. "What would I have done without *you*? I wouldn't be graduating early from Dallas Baptist University." Piper scurried to Angie and planted a big kiss on her cheek." With Mom, Dad, the twins, and Pierce in California, you were a life-saver. And, most of all, I wouldn't have met Brad."

Angie shed a few tears and held onto her granddaughter's tiny waist. Oh such youth. Where had all the time gone? Piper glowed with confidence and maturity.

"Come sit next to me a minute." Angie sank into the sofa, and plucked a piece of paper from the pages of Psalms in her favorite Bible. Her husband's obituary. "I hope Brad has a sense of humor like your grandfather."

Piper's gentle hand took the paper from her, and she read the words aloud.

Frederick Ansel Cooper bit the dust, sang sayonara on the steel guitar, and ate his last fried pie on April 1st, a perfect date for a recovering old codger and prankster to bid adieu. A retired bean counter, he was a self-proclaimed social bumble bee, meaning he was a social butterfly who fell prey to fashion faux pau-ism, often seen wearing knee high white socks, spandex stretched over a bulging tummy, and over-sized glasses from the 80s.

He loved God and served Him. Loved his family and reeked with affection for them. Loved coffee strong enough to make his teeth itch, poured ketchup on everything from eggs to applesauce, and cussed at the TV when the Cowboys didn't win. He disliked the color red, like in the lights he repeatedly ran, especially on the way to church.

"Ansey" credited his life-long happiness to his loving wife Angela Elizabeth Hemphill Cooper, their three perfect children Susan, Eric, and Todd, and seven stunning baby grands. He's survived by all of them, some incarcerated extended family, plus a few enemies from the IRS, and some seeking political asylum.

Ansey left a note saying, "Despite what you might think, I'm in heaven, so don't wear black to my service. See you soon, and to my best friend Hank, I'll see you a week from Thursday."

"I miss you, you ornery corker." Angie stood and forced a smile.

"I do, too, Grams. You and Gramps provided fun and demonstrated real faith, never that self-righteous kind. I didn't take the time to thank Gramps, but I want to thank you now." Piper's silvery blue eyes shone.

She gazed at Piper while memories of that chubby toddler, now a grown up, engaged young lady danced in her head. From the day she came home from the hospital, all pink and perfect, Piper had stolen her heart. Now Piper had advanced from being a member of the youth choir to directing the members. She marveled at this young woman she hopelessly admired. How had Piper accomplished all of this in the wink of an eye?

Her granddaughter scampered upstairs, words still tumbling out, but drifting from her earshot.

Angie loved her home in McKinney, Texas and had a stable life, a predictable one with plenty of church activities and friends. But her heart ached.

A familiar clicking on the dark hardwood floors jarred her attention.

"Come here, Zsa Zsa, my four-legged best friend." Zsa Zsa waggled her whole sandy blond and white body. "You miss him, too, don't cha? Ansey said he didn't like dogs, especially Shih Tzus, but you made a liar out of him, didn't you?" She picked up her small friend and squeezed. "He even named you." Tousling her dog's ruffled fur gave her a happy, nostalgic feeling. "You've been with me through thick and thin, and the *thin* barged in when Ansey died."

Zsa Zsa snuggled into her lap. Angie leaned back and closed her eyes.

Dear Lord, please help me. You gave me a wonderful husband once, and I deeply thank You. I don't need or want another one, but please take away this boulder of loneliness crushing my chest.

Zsa jumped onto the sofa. "That's right, girl, all I need is four legs and a tail."

Zsa Zsa gave a yap and wagged her bottom.

***

Jake Stewart slammed the ax into a large piece of wood on the ground and cracked the log open with one hard chop. He surveyed the expanse of land before him, his beloved Texas, stretching on forever. He especially loved the wide-open spaces Gunter provided, along with work, hobnobbing with nature, and solitude. Sometimes too much solitude though. His black Lab Bob sauntered nearby and swept a lazy tail.

At the sound of a horse's neighing, he startled. "Hello, Sam."

"You look busy, 'ol friend. Goldy and I just stopped by for a minute." Sam patted the horse.

Jake dug his ax into the thick branches. His woodpile grew.

"You're strong for an old fogy." Sam sent Jake a good-natured smile.

"Yeah, suppose so." Jake took another hit on a tree limb. "Being outside is good for ya. Don't miss those forty years cramped indoors. Loved being a CPA but don't miss the work one iota." He inhaled enough to take in half of Texas.

"You goin' to the dance in Old McKinney?" Sam had that know-what-you're-thinking stare he wore when trying to arrange Jake's life for him.

"Naaah, Don't think so."

"Do you suppose you're gonna meet some woman out here in the middle of nowhere with a bunch of cattle and other varmints?

"Maybe." Jake yanked up his ax and powered

down his arm to split open another log.

"Expect some woman to drop in your lap?"

"Now there's an idea." Jake peered upward a minute.

"In high school you could get any girl you wanted, but now you're gonna have to exert a little more effort, ya know." Sam squinted his raisin-colored eyes and wiped his hand over a mostly bald head sporting a thin white ring circling the dome. "Go dancin' Saturday night. You'll be glad you did." Sam shook the reins, and he and Goldy galloped off.

"Don't think so." Jake shouted after his friend.

He threw the logs on the pile, wiped his forehead with a handkerchief, and pulled the ringing cell phone from his pants pocket.

"Hi, Brad. Nothing much. Sure, I can pick up Piper and her grandmother. What's her name? Mrs. Cooper? Yeah, in about an hour, give or take fifteen minutes. I'll chauffer them to the engagement party with time to spare. You keep studying for the bar. I'm proud of ya, son."

Jake smiled. He loved to help out his grandson. Jumped at the chance to see Brad. Always been a good boy, and now with lightening speed, he'd become a good man. His son's son.

Brad shared his love for the land. Another reason Brad held a special place in Jake's heart. Brad loved fishing and hunting too. So much in common.

With his gloved hands Jake brushed off leaves

and wood pieces and took off. His long legs made for a quick jaunt past giant live oaks and pecan trees and across an acre of his property to the back door of his ranch-style home. Bob scampered ahead barking.

***

He showered and shaved in record time, hitched on his new Levis, white shirt, and navy sports coat. Wanted to look nice for his new granddaughter-in-law-to-be and for the rest of the family he'd see later. Pulled on his cowboy boots. He grabbed his keys from their hanger in the laundry room, and jumped into his Ford Taurus. His seventeen year-old-car was in great condition, and he loved the thing. Didn't cotton to getting new cars just because of the date on their chassis.

"Bye, Bob, take care of things while I'm gone!"

***

Jake sped down Highway 289 enjoying fresh air from his half-open window and the white dusting of snow along open fields. He fumbled for his sunglasses to block the brightness of this sunny but frigid day.

Lord, I've been awfully lonely since Sophie died five years ago. I know I'm a stubborn old cuss... but with a sense of humor. I love my children and grandkids, all sixteen of them, but they have their own lives. Sam's right. I don't know how to meet women. Whata Ya say, Lord? Drop somebody in my lap?

He pulled up to the curb of a red brick home, trimmed in white stone. One giant live oak canopied the small front yard, yielding the only sign of green in this neat, well-kept, but not-over-the-top neighborhood. Brad's directions proved to be perfect. No trouble finding Piper's grandmother's house.

Piper's a good girl. Good head on her shoulders. She'd be great for Brad. Her artistic personality balanced his serious-minded, all-work-and-little-play grandson.

He checked his hair in the rearview mirror and eased out of the car.

"Why did I glance at my hair? I'm not a teenager. What should I say to Piper's grandmother? A lady of what…eighty probably. Ring the doorbell, you crazy old coot."

***

Angie glanced up. Her oldest granddaughter never walked. High energy propelled her into a half-run everywhere these days.

"Hey, Grams!" Piper swung into the living room. Her cheeks flushed with excitement, her blue eyes bigger than should be allowed. Her brown hair swirled in soft curls at her shoulders.

"Hey, yourself." She hoped her smile hid her watery eyes. "I'm ready for your engagement party. Well, almost. And on Valentine's Day too. Honey, move your gift over, closer to the door. Brad can carry that big box to the car for us. I'll be back in a jiffy. Just need to touch up my makeup."

"Sure, Grams, but hurry. Brad will be here any minute to drive us to the party. And, you look great. Always do. You look like that lady I saw on TV reruns. You know with your same first name? *Angie* something." Piper straightened her pink sweater and slipped into her shoes.

"You mean Angie Dickinson?" Angie's nose crinkled. "Yeah, right! I want your rose-colored glasses."

"You do look like her, but with green eyes. Same blond hair. Now, hurry, Grams." Piper waved arms and smiled.

"I won't keep your fiancé waiting." Angie tweaked Piper's button nose and headed to her bedroom.

The doorbell rang, and the door creaked open. A male voice mingled with Piper's giggles.

The voice sounded like Brad, but deeper. A bass version of Piper's intended.

Angie powdered her nose, slipped on her heels, and grabbed her black and gray bag.

Dear God, I'm ecstatic for Piper and Brad. I miss Ansey's laughter and company but, Lord, I'm ready to be independent, to establish myself in a career. People tell me I have the knack for decorating. I certainly have the love for it. And since I went from my parent's home to one with my husband, I'm bent on standing alone. Not be dependent on anyone ever again. A career is just the ticket. Right, Lord?

She rounded the corner to her living room,

patted Zsa Zsa good-bye, caught her heel in a nick in the hardwood, and fell head-long into two strong arms. Her strand of pearls popped and spewed their fake little orbs all over the floor. She wobbled. Her lipstick swished across the stranger's white shirt.

She gazed up into the warmest espresso-colored eyes she'd ever seen. His shoulders looked like load-bearing beams on the Atchison, Topeka, and Santa Fe. A full crop of dark, curly hair with slight shades of silver at both temples graced his perfect head. A crooked smile broke onto his face. A square jaw sported a cleft chin. This wasn't her granddaughter's fiancé. Who was he? Was this heaven? He was a perfect specimen, except for his muddy cowboy boots. Close enough to perfection anyway.

Zsa Zsa dropped her chew toy, leaving her pink tongue peaking out from her mouth, her body heaving with hard breaths, her tail swishing the floor. She stared at this tower of a man and whimpered.

I know what you mean, Zsa, I know what you mean.

Chapter 2

Jake steadied the woman he held, and his eyes swept upward. Not his lap, but his arms. *Close enough, Lord.*

"Oh, Mr. Stewart...." Piper rushed over.

In all of his years he'd never had a woman fall into his arms. He pondered this about one whole second. He liked it.

"Grams, are you okay? What happened? I mean really, Grams." Piper's soft words grew louder, and her eyes widened as the lady pried herself from his arms. Piper's pretty face blushed crimson.

"Oh dear, I tripped on something. I'm so sorry." The woman's face reddened and she hung onto his arm.

"Grams, this is Mr. Stewart, Brad's grandfather. He's come to take us to the engagement party. Brad's held up at school."

"Hi, Brad's grandfather. I mean Mr. Stewart." She brushed herself off and cleared her throat.

"Jake, please. Jake Stewart. Nice to hold ya, I mean meetcha. You're Piper's *grandmother*?"

***

Angie drank in the homey atmosphere of Brad's Aunt Janie's house. Pink floral wallpaper flanked the miniscule dining area. A crystal punch bowl, poised on top of a mahogany table, sparkled. She hadn't seen a punch bowl in twenty years. What she could do to update this quaint cottage-style home. Visions of soft blues and apricots floated in her head.

Such a lovely engagement party, but Angie's brain replayed the picture of Brad's gorgeous grandfather. His melodious, bass voice and low-pitched chuckles tickled her fancy. "Be still, my heart." Laughter, beautiful gifts, and marriage advice from Piper's friends who'd been married all of six months to two years couldn't keep her from fixating on Mr. Wonderful. She *shouldn't* allow such thoughts about a man who wasn't her husband. How could she delete these messages?

Sweet-toned voices provided music of a successful day, but her thoughts returned to Jake. Her heart fluttered again. Stop that. Did anyone see her peering outside? Just one more glance and she'd be finished with him. She was a grown woman with three children and seven grandchildren. A grown woman? She was sort of *old* by some standards. So why did her heart dance like a teenager's and her stomach flitter like it held caged butterflies? She needed to leave. Her head swam. She'd tell Piper she was coming down with something but couldn't admit the mysterious ailment reeked of puppy love. A ridiculous happenstance.

Angie leaned against a wall in the cozy living room, munching on a tea cake, and patting her mouth with a pink cloth napkin.

"A penny for your thoughts." Her longtime friend Dixie-Lee, born in Charleston, aptly named for a head-to-toe Southern Belle, dripped with elongated syllables, carried monogrammed hankies, spoke drawn-out *y'alls and darlins,* drank sweet tea on her veranda, and declared biscuits not served with milk gravy a grievous sin.

"It's been quite a day, hasn't it? So much fun watching Piper and Brad's pals pile her with love. I'm so glad our granddaughters are best buds." Angie stole one more peek through the window.

Dixie-Lee whispered, "Say, darlin', why don't you come to the dance in Old McKinney with Bill and me tomorrow night? Just might meet somebody interesting." Her friend's graceful fingers nudged Angie's shoulder, and she smiled.

"Oh, no, thank you. I have a good book to read, and our Book Club meets Tuesday. I'm happy with my memories." She extracted herself from her friend's grip and shot her a grin she didn't feel.

Did she sound convincing or like she made excuses? A man she'd known about an hour had turned her world upside down. She'd put a stop to those crazy feelings.

"Yes, I've heard all this before, but I know you, Angie, and I care about you. You need someone so..."

"So...so? What? I'm happy with my life. You don't know everything about me."

"Yes, that's true, but I understand a lot about you, and I'm sure you need to get out and hobnob. Did you hear socializing is good for your brain health? I went to a lecture..."

"Reading is also good for brain health. I read too. Ansey was the best. Can't replace him, and don't want to."

"Think about what I've said. I'll call you tomorrow." Dixie-Lee offered her a cup of punch.

She sipped her drink. Old fashioned punch made with Ginger Ale and lime sherbet. Brought back memories of her one and only wedding shower. She'd be fine tomorrow night at home with her book. She threw a tiny wave to her friend.

She twisted around in time to bump into Piper. "Hi, honey."

"Come with me, Grams." With flawless flair and perfect finesse Piper swung her from one group of friends and Brad's family to another.

Angie dropped into a chair of oversized softness. Her gaze crept toward the window. Their white blanket of snow had melted, giving way to brown lawns and flickering street lights. Silver clouds, perched in a hazy coral and periwinkle sky, whispered a nostalgic good-bye to another Valentine's Day. A shadow of sadness swallowed her. Giggles trickled from all corners of the house.

From across the old-fashioned living room, Piper motioned.

She inhaled deeply, rose, and scrambled to a group of Brad's family.

"Yes, I know what you mean, Earlene. Can't believe our little Piper Elizabeth, my sweet first-born granddaughter, is all grown up and getting married. Yes, *Elizabeth* is named for me. I've always been so proud she shares my name. Piper's always been a good girl and uses her talent of singing and playing the piano and violin to honor God." She turned toward Brad's mother Grace. "She's exhibited great wisdom in choosing a husband too. An answer to prayer."

Grace's eyes glistened.

"We feel the same way about Piper." Grace hugged her granddaughter.

Angie's heart thumped. "I just wish Piper's mom could be here. Susan was sick she couldn't get away from San Diego, but she and the rest of the family will arrive in a few months. Huge thanks to your daughter for an exquisite party. Finding pink tulips: extraordinary."

Car lights flooded the front yard.

She inhaled air, hoping not to hyperventilate. She could imagine the headlines: Grandmother Splats on the Floor with Heart Attack. Who'd believe the cause: a man?

The doorbell hit blood-curdling decibels.

Her breathing ceased. Her whole body dripped

in nervous sweat, and her legs wobbled.

The door creaked open. A long, sleeved arm reached out to hug Brad's mother.

"Brad!" Piper's squeal could be heard by all the dogs from there to Oklahoma.

Jake followed, a tall, slinky redhead wrapped around his muscular arm as tight as a bean burrito on Cinco de Mayo. A slithery smile curled her lips.

Jealousy plucked at Angie's heart and poked her head with sharp, evil darts. She didn't want to want Jake, but he surely should've wanted her.

Chapter 3

Angie squirmed and stretched her legs to the new morning. She propped herself higher in her king-size bed and slipped her sage green and blue polka-dot granny glasses between the pages of a book. She gripped a telephone in her left hand, and patted her hair caught in a scrunchy holding a short pony tail on top of her head.

"No, my sweet Dixie-Lee, I don't want to go to the dance in Old McKinney. I don't think so. Yes, I understand, you want what's best for me, honey. Can't put down Anne Greene's *Angel With Steel Wings*. My Book Club is gonna discuss this novel next week. Did you know there were female test pilots in WWII? Neither did I. See you in choir tomorrow. Right now I need coffee. Bye, hon."

***

Angie stopped in front of a one-story, white house with steel-gray shutters and a sweeping veranda, a famous residence in McKinney. This homestead had dated back to 1875, according to the historic yard sign. Children no doubt had raced through the grassy lawn, climbed the towering trunks of live oaks, and dangled from their gnarly branches.

She pulled into the already crowded parking area. Strands of clear lights twinkled from the roof of the outdoor deck. She maneuvered her SUV into the spot, turned off the ignition, and nudged herself out.

The clear sky shone with lustrous stars. Surely this phenomenon of the stars at night being big and bright belonged exclusively to Texas. Well, maybe not.

She approached the front door. What was she doing here? She'd told Dixie-Lee in no uncertain terms she wouldn't attend this dance and she didn't want to meet a man. But here she stood at that very shindig.

She'd persevere thirty minutes. She could appease Dixie-Lee's obsession, yet not remain long enough to get bored, or embarrass herself by not being asked to dance. This was just like high school. Nerve-wracking.

On second thought...she turned on her heel.

Out of the cold, fresh air rang the unmistakable voice of Dixie-Lee. Angie spun around and conked her head on the forehead of her best friend. Dixie-Lee's alto voice, a cross between Jo Anne Worley's and Ethel Merman's bounced through the crisp air. "Oh, Angie, dear." Her friend rubbed her head.

"Oh, hi. I changed my mind. I have to go." Angie clutched her purse and hot-footed it toward the steps.

Dixie-Lee looped her arm through Angie's. "Come in for fifteen minutes. Some of our church friends are here. Have some hot cocoa with whipped cream on top. It's delish," Dixie-Lee fluttered thick, false eyelashes. The overhead lights caught the shimmer of red in her chin-length dark hair that swayed with her excited movements. Her five-foot-nine statuesque chum led Angie inside.

Buck Owens' *Act Naturally* chinked from the live band.

That was an interesting musical message. She didn't have a clue how to act any way but uncomfortable.

"Hi, Angie." A friend from Sunday School coaxed her to the hot cocoa and assorted sweets.

She lingered with the group. Dixie-Lee dropped anchor close by.

"My allergies are acting up, so I'm never going to be able to sing *How Great Thou Art* in choir on Sunday." Pretty redhead Jillian Pierce held her throat and rolled her eyes.

"Sure you can. I wonder if the Swedish author Carl Boberg had any idea when he wrote his poem that it would reach such heights in popularity?" Hedda, a chubby brunette smiled.

Despite the caffeine in the hot chocolate and chocolate chip cookies, Angie relaxed and began to enjoy herself. She dropped her purse on a chair.

When *He'll Have to Go* wafted through the crowd with lights glimmering and friends laughing, Angie's heart strings drooped. Jim Reeves' song poked a stiff message in her face.

A voice from the veranda thundered, "Grab your partners!"

"Time to go. I'm not about to do-si-do." Angie scanned the tables for her purse and waved to Dixie-Lee.

"Be my partner." Five-foot-four inch Zigfeld Bean, better know as Ziggy, took her hand and yanked her toward the outside. He was too good a friend to decline. A widower, he hadn't missed a social event in the last five years.

If only she'd worn flats instead of these two-inch heels. Ziggy clamped her waist, and she stared over his head. They began their promenade.

The caller's deep voice vibrated commands and kept them swirling. What must they have looked like allemanding left and do-si-doing, and shooting the star? Folks from their fifties to eighty-something, with tummies protruding, patches of hair bouncing, and some slick heads shining. She enjoyed this falderal after all. She hadn't embarrassed herself either, because no one paid attention to her. If only she'd learned this lesson earlier in life. Most people were too busy thinking about themselves to give a rip about her.

About the time she realized she hadn't seen Ziggy Bean in a while and heaved a deep breath, a firm arm latched onto her. She gazed up and up, past an ample chest and broad shoulders. Then she plunged right smack toward the face of...Jake Stewart. He gave her a courtesy turn and promenaded her off the dance floor.

"It's good to see you, Mrs. Cooper." Jake's chest surged like he was out of breath. "How about if we find a chair and sit down?"

She scanned the area. "I was dancing with somebody, but don't know where he went."

"Yeah, it's easy to lose somebody in this crowd. I'm sorry, did you come with a date?" Jake's onyx eyes sparkled, then narrowed.

Would he be sad if she had a date? "No, not really. Ziggy Bean asked me to dance, but I seemed to have misplaced him. And, please call me Angie."

"Who? *Ziggy...Bean*?" Jake's eyes bore a glint as he pronounced Ziggy's name. "Well, maybe Mr. Bean wouldn't mind if we sat down and chatted a minute."

"Are you with a date?" She held her breath and scoured the vicinity for *Miss Slithery Redhead*.

"No. I'm here with my friend, Sam." He angled his glance to the door. "There are some chairs inside." Jake held the door for her. As she slipped by him she noticed Ziggy with a petite brunette. Maybe he'd finally met someone. Her heart beamed.

She took a seat at a small table, and Jake joined her.

"Having fun?" Jake's dark eyes glimmered.

How did he always smile with his eyes?

"Surprisingly, yes."

"Me, too. I hadn't planned to come, but a persistent friend got the best of me." Jake retrieved two glasses of water for them.

"I know what you mean." She sipped her cool drink.

"I've been thinking about you since we met a few weeks ago." Jake's voice grew husky.

Could he see her heart leap? What was he thinking about her? She may have grinned but wasn't sure.

"May I take you out to lunch tomorrow after church?"

"Aaa. Some of us in the choir go out together every Sunday." Her heartbeat quickened.

"Well, how about later...dinner?"

"I have plans."

"Dinner on Monday then."

"Can't."

"Tuesday? My women's group *Silly Saints* meets."

"How about coffee on Wednesday morning?'

"Bible study."

"Thursday?"

"Coffee?" Her palms sweated.

"At Deep in the Heart of Texas."

"Around the corner from my house. Well, I guess so."

"Great. What's your phone number?"

"I don't know." Her drawl dragged a little.

"What?"

"I mean I had to change my number. Oh, yeah, I remember." She tore a piece of paper from a notepad in her purse, then jotted down the number. When was the last time she'd given her number to a man for a date? Was having coffee a date or an outing?

"I'll pick you up at...? Are you an early riser?"

"Not too."

"I'll pick you up at ten."

What about *Miss-Wrap-Around-Your-Arm-as-Tight-as-an-Ace-Bandage*? "Okay, but I'll meet you there. I have errands in the afternoon."

"If you're sure."

Was this a date? What was she doing?

"Thursday at ten?" Her voice detached itself from her brain, and she perspired from head to toe.

Chapter 4

Angie blossomed in the beauty and energy rampant in Emmaline's Brunch and Bakery.

Her best bud Dixie-Lee wiggled into her high-backed chair beside her.

"I need this monthly excursion to boost my happy meter. Having fun, Dixie-Lee?" Angie scanned the group of women who proudly referred to themselves as *Silly Saints* as they visited and giggled while seated at lace-clothed tables.

"Yes. Aren't we glad these ladies followed their children and grandchildren here to Dallas so we'd have an excuse to meet, eat, and laugh together? Now we're one crazy group of grannies." Dixie-Lee turned and waved. "Hi, Pam, hi, Linda!"

Dixie-Lee gleefully raved about something right through our fearless leader Roxanne's opening and prayer.

Angie sneaked a bite of golden hash browns and a biscuit swimming in milk gravy.

Dixie-Lee nodded at Angie's food, no doubt her

southern approval.

"Now, tell me everything. I witnessed you and great-looking-Jake huddled together at the dance last weekend." Dixie-Lee nudged her and stared straight into her eyes.

"Just a minute, hon. They're singing birthday songs to the March *babies*."

"C'mon, Angie. What are you keeping from me? I'm gonna bust a gut." Her friend tapped her hand.

"Hon, I'm gonna miss another joke. Just a minute."

Hattie Pearl stood, her deep-set eyes sparkling, cotton-colored hair framing her face hosting crinkles at her eyes and mouth. "Ladies...."

"But, you've gotta tell me." Dixie-Lee spoke in Angie's ear.

"Dix, hold on."

"A few words to the wise, the only normal people you know...are the ones you don't know well." The crowd giggled, and Hattie Pearl smiled. "And studies show that women with a little extra meat on their bones live longer than the men...who mention it." More laughter. She slipped into her seat.

Dixie-Lee leaned over. "Don't you love her? I want to be just like her when I grow up...or get to be eighty-six. She's beautiful and has all her crayons in the box."

"Yes, I do. Love her name. Should be in a novel." Angie squeezed her friend's hand. "Well, I do want to talk to you but not sure this is the right place."

"Sure it is. Nobody's listening."

"Not much to tell really...except Jake asked me out." Her face went hot.

A scream walloped the air. Dixie-Lee covered her mouth.

A few women peered at them.

"What? And you didn't call me immediately, your very best friend?" Dixie-Lee's voice rode the roller coaster of sound until she gained control and simmered down.

"There's not much to tell. He asked me to dinner, and I said no." Angie sipped her last drop of orange juice and clanked her glass back on the table.

"You said what? Now, listen here, he's the best thing that's come along since fried chicken and pecan pie. You get right on that cell phone and tell him you'd lapsed into insanity, but you've come to your senses now and want to go." Dixie-Lee's sky blue eyes enlarged, and her face flushed bright red.

"Don't have a conniption." She gave her friend's arm a gentle squeeze. "I said no to dinner, but yes to having coffee Thursday morning at *Deep in the Heart of Texas*. I'm regretting that decision though."

"Well, don't. Get dressed to kill and don a rapturous smile. And, wear your crimson, suede high-heeled boots. You'll snap his chaps. I mean your expensive dressy boots, not the cowgirl ones."

"I knew what you meant."

"Don't show up in that raggedy black sweater Cora June gave you last year either. Black pulls your face down. Blondes need lighter, bright colors, and men love red, even if the color is on your feet."

"Ansey didn't like red."

"Because of all the tickets he got for running red lights." Dixie-Lee bumped Angie's shoulder and grinned.

"You're making my head swim. And that sweater is not raggedy. Just so you know, people have told me I look great in black. Really, Dixie-Lee."

"Well, they lied, darlin'."

"Sunshine flooded through the pastel pink curtains on long windows, and smiles bloomed on every face there.

"Ladies, in honor of St. Patrick's Day on the 17th, we have shamrocks on the tables and Irish sayings on them, so get ready to share!

Rachel beamed, "No man wore a scarf as warm as his daughter's arm around his neck."

"An Irishman has an abiding sense of tragedy which sustains him through temporary periods of joy."

Angie leaned toward Dixie-Lee. "I come by my melancholy naturally."

"I know. Me, too."

"Here's mine," Margo, a slim redhead, crooned.

May the love and laughter light your days and

warm your heart and home

May good and faithful friends be yours wherever you may roam.

Dixie-Lee pinched the whey out of Angie's arm, and stormed on with some of her own sayings, Irish and southern, and forged into more advice about dating.

Hattie Pearl stood again, her ebony eyes glistening. "My first husband passed away after forty years. His death broke my heart, but I consoled myself that I'd had a great marriage. Then the Lord brought another man into my life. Next month Hank and I will be married ten years. My first mother-in-law advised me to remarry if I could. It's never too late to love again."

"Would our hero steer you wrong?" Dixie-Lee held up her glass of juice to Hattie Pearl.

Angie wasn't interested. She could only love one man.

Why had she told Jake she'd have coffee with him Thursday?

Chapter 5

The day began without Angie's permission. Totally God's idea to raise the sun. She awoke before dawn with her heart racing and her head pounding. Five cups of coffee and four hours later she'd returned to bed with a pillow over her head. What had she done? She couldn't meet a man for coffee, or for anything else. Her heart yearned to see Jake, but her head reminded her she loved Ansey. Wanting to see Jake drenched heavy doses of guilt on her too. The cold, hard fact remained that she wasn't married anymore, and that truth tortured her.

She'd call Jake to cancel.

***

She grabbed her red purse and slung a long strap over her shoulder, slid out of the car, and heaved a deep breath. Her red flats clicked on the pavement. Okay, she'd worn red, but not the sky-high boots Dixie-Lee had advised. She'd hoped the long crimson scarf looped around her neck provided the right amount of bright color against her black sweater and pants. She pressed her hands across her waist and felt a bump. Shouldn't have eaten that biscuit and gravy on Tuesday.

Inside *Deep in the Heart of Texas* her gaze darted past the giant star of Texas on the rock wall and landed on Jake sitting at a small table. When their eyes met, he smiled that all encompassing grin that lit his face and her heart. She loved the warmth he exuded and needed it too.

Jake stood and took her hands in his toasty, brawny grasp.

Everything about him gave her goose bumps.

Jake held a chair for her. "I'm glad you're here. They have great muffins and bear claws. I've checked them out. But, the coffee's brutal."

Angie stubbed her toe as she fell into her seat. "I'll have some herb tea. I'm *coffeed* out." Her head throbbed from her morning deluge of caffeine. Ansey loved bear claws. Was that a man-thing? Those must host a zillion calories per bite.

Jake dropped into his chair and signaled to the waitress.

"I'll have some Earl Grey and a blueberry muffin, please." Why did she order a muffin?

"Tell me about yourself." He threw her the look that made her heart leap.

"Well, I'm Angela Elizabeth Hemphill Cooper. Mother of three and grandmother of seven. I have sons, Eric, in Austin and Todd in Allen. Our daughter Susan and her family are moving back to

Dallas in a couple of months after a stint in California. The boys have two children a piece, and Susan has three. Now, tell me about you." She drummed up all her nerve to look him straight in his seductive, dark eyes.

His gaze sent cold sweat prickling all over her body and excitement sizzling in her chest.

Resonant words slid from his mouth. "I'm Jacob Jefferson Stewart. I also have three children, two boys–Jake Jr. and William—and our baby Julianne, and ten grandchildren, all close by. When I was in the Air Force I lived in Europe and California, then later in New York City. Lived in Dallas for a while but moved to Gunter about ten years ago."

"You've lived in some interesting places. What do you do, or did you do, for a living?"

"Anything with numbers. A statistician, a CPA, and in banking finance. Been retired six years."

"I've lived in McKinney so long...like when people left apple pies cooling on their windowsills, families had supper together every night, and no one considered any place but church on Sunday morning. I can't imagine anywhere else." An excited giggle leapt into her throat and spilled out.

"Know what you mean. Love those memories. Between all the moves around the country, I dropped into Gunter as often as I could." Jake's mouth crinkled into a boyish grin. "Born there and I wanted to come back. True that when ya live in a small town, your mama knows your latest prank before you walk through the front door, but I've always loved the rural life."

"Me, too." Happiness percolated throughout her body.

"You could skip rocks on the creek, ride your bike to school, go to church with your teachers, and know people working hard before sun-up and past sundown. They have leathery skin, and their reward was a lot more respect than money." Jake's voice played a rhapsody on the keyboard of her heart.

Jake's cell phone rang. He glanced at the screen, pressed a button, and turned back to Angie. "Do you remember those signs along the highways when we were kids? Some kinds of shaving advertisements." Jake relaxed against his chair.

"Burma Shave? I loved those. Let's see if I can conjure one up in my brain. Aaaa, 'No, no...she said...to her bristly beau...I'd rather...eat the mistletoe.'"

Jake chuckled. "Remember, 'Toughest...whiskers...in the town...we hold 'em up...you mow 'em down'"? A grin sped across his face.

Thanks to Jake, hidden memories of fun laughed into her present.

Jake's cheeks flushed. "So, Angela Elizabeth Hemphill Cooper, what do you like to do for fun?" That forever mischievous, endearing glint danced in Jake's eyes again.

"I like movies." She sipped her tea.

"Me, too."

"And I loved the dance in Old McKinney, but don't do that often."

"Me, too."

"I love the Cowboys and the Mavericks."

"Me, too. Sounds like you and I drink from the same trough."

"Oh, I love singing in the church choir."

"Now, that I've never done." Jake leaned forward. "I'd love to hear you sing some time."

Her face went hot.

"Are you outdoorsy?"

"Not too. I've decided exercise is a myth conjured up by the hopelessly fit." Angie smiled.

His cell phone lit up again. He pressed a button. The phone darkened.

Should she drop the bomb, if it would be a bomb, that she wasn't interested in a long term commitment?

"You lit up when you mentioned family. Was your family close when you were growing up?" Jake peered right into her heart.

She studied the remnants of her muffin. "I wish that had been the case. I was close to my mother her whole life. But when I was eight, my father sat me down, and told me not to ever call him Daddy again. Said he wasn't my father. From then on when the family went on vacations, I stayed with my grandparents, my mother's parents." Hot coals smoldered inside her.

"When I gathered all my nerve, I went to Mother and told her what he'd said. Her face turned as gray as a somber day. Between sobs Mother confessed that my biological father was a man she'd fallen in love with in her home state of North Dakota when she was sixteen. His family nixed their marriage, saying he was too young, and they paid for Mother to move here to Texas, and she never heard from any of them again. Her parents moved with her."

"I'm so sorry. I didn't mean to open old wounds. I just didn't think...."

"It's okay. I can't believe I spilled all of this to you. I've never told anyone else except Ansey. Not even Dixie-Lee or any of my children know."

"You don't have to tell me any more."

"Well, the good news is that the love of Jesus filled that abyss. I dashed headlong into the arms of Christ and never looked back. I did whatever I could to bathe my children and Ansey in my love."

A smile walked across Jake's face.

Guilt and regret blindsided her. Why had she admitted her dirty laundry to this stranger?

"How old were you when you accepted Christ?" Jake leaned closer.

"Seventeen. Saw Billy Graham on TV, knelt down right there in my grandparents' living room and prayed to receive Him."

"And you?"

"I was twenty-five when I went to a church revival. I'd decided I was ready to admit I was a sinner and couldn't save myself, so I gave my life to Jesus. Wished they still had those meetings." Jake's eyes sparkled.

***

Jake glanced at his watch and shook it.

"What's the matter?"

"Nothing, did you know we've been here five hours?"

Angie tinkled her spoon as she placed it on the saucer with the cup.

Jake took her hand.

How perfectly her hand fit in his. Could such a fine man as Jake Stewart love her? Ansey had, but maybe Jake thought she was not worth messing with like her stepfather Ralph and her biological father. Could she be wrong about needing a career and not wanting to get involved with anyone? Maybe Jake was a gift from God, like Ansey had been.

"Angie, I've enjoyed our time together." He straightened his shoulders. "I'd like to take you out tomorrow for dinner."

"I don't know." Should she tell him she had other plans for her life which didn't include commitments? Why did he touch her heart with his eyes and make her stomach flip-flop? "I need to tell you something."

"Will tomorrow be okay? I just realized I have an appointment in fifteen minutes." He motioned for the waitress.

"Sure." Telling him she wasn't interested could

wait, but should she tell him over dinner when he was paying?

Chapter 6

Jake's massive hand enclosed hers, giving Angie's heart a tingle. She'd never been to this restaurant before. Jake's idea. Despite a sweltering day, their ride to Celina left cool, calming delight swirling in her head. He held the door, and she entered Evie Jo's Café, the giant ceiling fans swirling.

"Welcome, y'all. Come this way." A middle-aged woman in a diner-logoed tee shirt and flowy denim skirt tickling the tops of her boots winked and smiled. "Hi, Jake."

He nodded and turned back to Angie.

Angie slid into the only empty booth in the place. Jake's grinning face shone across the table from her, and he reached for her hand.

The hostess pitched the menus to them and scuffled off.

As she scanned the rustic square room, her heart fluttered. "I bet all this wall paraphernalia could tell some great stories." Her gaze passed some spurs, a wagon wheel, and an old Texas license plate on the natural wood walls. Yellowed menus displaying bygone prices of six-cent soft drinks and fifteen-cent sundaes, and ropes draped lasso-style triggered sweet recollections.

Jake pointed to a far wall. "That wheel reminds me of my grandfather's old buggy. I spent many an hour tooling around with him. Hey, Gene Autry and Roy Rogers are three booths down," Jake boomed.

Dwight Eisenhower hung framed and smiling right smack at eye level to her left. "Jake, do you think the president ate here?"

"Maybe. He was born up in Denison. Could've come to his old stomping grounds."

"Remember the campaign button *I like Ike*?" She surveyed the walls of memories. "Did you know his brothers were also called Ike?"

"Ya mean like, 'Meet my brother Horace, and my other brother Horace?'"

Jake always made her laugh. She loved people who found humor in ordinary circumstances. Loved? Oh, dear, she meant liked.

His phone lit up. He released her hand, checked the screen, and punched a side button.

No sooner had they ordered fried catfish and fries than a stocky man, microphone in hand, bellowed over jivey background music. "I see one of our favorite guests is here. All you regulars know who I'm talking about! Help me welcome our very own Jake Stewart to lead our singing!"

Patrons beat their hands on tables, and a

spotlight out of nowhere fell on her date.

He looked around, smiled, and waved. He didn't budge.

More clapping and drum-rolling.

"Come on, Jake! Your fans await!" The microphoned man stood before them, flapping his burly arms, nodding a mostly bald head, and grinning like he'd discovered the pot of gold at the end of a rainbow.

Her excitement soared with the crowd's.

He rose and swaggered to the middle of the café, the bright light following him, along with everyone's gaze.

Would his melodic deep voice send chills up and down the spines of the other women there? She braced herself. Her hands perspired. Her chest swelled.

"Now, gang, I've played the harmonica for ya but I don't sing."

"I bet you do." popped up from one side of the room.

"We believe in you" chimed from the other side.

"Well, if you insist, but y'all have to follow along." Jake glanced toward someone in back. "Do you know something by the Beach Boys?"

"Sure do."

Excitement flooded the room.

He threw his head back and his arms up.

The lights dimmed. The room fell silent.

She held her breath.

He gripped the mic. Canned music burst forth. Big, beautiful Jake sang into the microphone. But, instead of music caressing her senses, adenoidal racket pierced the ozone. What just happened? Where was that noise coming from?

Various verses sprang from his strangled up-tempo. His adagio drooped and his falsetto fumbled with the tonal quality of twenty-three tin cans clanging behind a '62 Buick. If the Beach Boys got wind of this, they'd surely call the police.

He dropped his hand, and his jubilant jamboree ended as the crowd erupted into applause. He wrangled a grin that covered his face.

He bowed, and bowed again.

From another table someone muttered. "We love him, but he couldn't carry a tune in a fat man's bathtub."

The houselights sprang to life, and claps and yahoos shook the walls.

He sported a sheepish grin but waved.

After a couple of lengthy strides, Jake halted beside her.

What should she say? She squirmed.

A tall redhead pounced on Jake. A peevish whine curdled the air. "There you are. I had a feeling you'd be here." The wrap-around woman from the engagement party swooped in and stole into Jake's arms. "Jakey, I've been calling you. You bad boy. You never answered." She nestled to his chest.

Miss Lanky Swanky met Angie's gaze, inhaled

from her toes, sighed, and plastered a grin on her made-up face. "Oh, hi. I'm Penelope Penbrook, but everyone who's anyone calls me Buffie. That's the name I was given when I was a deb. Remember, Jakey?" She purred at him, then turned toward Angie and stuck out her long, pale hand.

Angie's heart beat faster. "Nice to meet you...aaa...Ms Penbrook."

"Please call me Buffie."

She smiled. "Thank you, Buffie."

Penelope Penbrook wormed closer to Jake and planted a kiss on his cheek. A coral splash smeared his face. "Am I still gonna see you tomorrow night?"

Jake stammered something.

Did he say yes?

How could he make a date with that woman right in front of her? Angie's mother had warned her about men's wandering eyes. Ansey had been the only exception. She jumped up. "I must go. And I see you have things to do, Mr. Stewart. Thank you for supper and for a...a...delightful evening." Well, up until five minutes ago.

"Bye, hon. See you soon." Buffie fluttered her eyes.

The clinging vine's words spewed flames of anger, tangled with embarrassment, throughout Angie's body.

"But, Angie, wait, wait. How...where are you going?"

"My head is pounding. I see my old friend

Ziggy. He'll take me home. Sorry. I have to go." She wheeled around.

"Angie, I really want to...."

Buffie-Muffie hugged Jake.

She'd never let down her guard again. Yes, all she needed was a design career and four furry paws to make her life complete. She had the profession and just the Shih Tzu she needed.

She lunged toward her pal. "Hey, Zig!"

Chapter 7

Angie's cell phone beeped. Caller ID read Jacob Stewart. How long must she ignore him to get the point across? He was history. Her face burned every time her thoughts returned to that day when she confessed her childhood misery to him...a stranger. And then his arm-in-arm display with the redhead at Evie Jo's. The childhood neglect dropped on her by unloving fathers should've stayed where the monster belonged—in her hidden past. Not to mention her stepfather's womanizing. Maybe Jake couldn't stay faithful to one woman either. Good riddance to him and Miss Penelope Penbrook, debutante. She had better things to fill her time. She deleted Jake's text, message unseen. He would never humiliate her again.

***

Jake chunked his phone onto the living room couch and plopped down. This technology was supposed to be *smart.*

What a stubborn woman. Angela Cooper was going to take some finesse. What could he say to her when he saw her again? He should've told her right there at the coffee shop he had no romantic interest in Buffie. How could he have said that with the perpetrator dangling from his arm? Angie's worth fighting for. He needed a strategy to reach her, and he'd have a heart-to-heart with Buffie.

Chapter 8

Angie slumped onto her family room couch with the day's events swimming in her head. Caring for others at the homeless shelter proved to be an exhausting business. Nevertheless, she loved the people and wanted to make a difference in their lives. Had she today?

Did she have enough energy to open a can of soup for dinner? Not sure.

"Hi, Grams. Bye, Grams." Piper scooped her into a tight hug and gave her a kiss. "Brad just drove up. Be back by midnight."

"Have fun."

The lock clasped in the door.

She couldn't muster the energy to amble to the pantry for some soup. The doorbell chimed, again and again.

What did Piper forget this time, besides her key? She took a deep breath, trudged to the living room, and flung open the front door. "Now, honey, what did you forget? Oh!"

"I like being called honey. Been called worse." Jake Stewart's brawny figure stood over her, while he smiled that infectious smile. "Don't close the door...please. I can explain."

She wasn't about to let him complicate her life. But why did her heart flutter and her toes curl under?

"I'm really tired, and I don't think we have anything to talk about." Angie gazed high enough to peer into Jake Stewart's dark eyes. He filled her doorway.

"I can explain. If I can't convince you to change your mind in five minutes, I'll leave."

Exhaustion bore down on her shoulders, but this giant's energy permeated the room and sneaked into her body, rousing something inside her. She bit her lip. Without thinking, she opened the door wider.

He stepped inside.

She motioned him to a chair in the living room. If only she'd brushed her hair in the last hour and put on lipstick, but then, why did she care? After five minutes, she'd never see him again. He couldn't say anything to fix things.

His body dwarfed her French chair, and his long legs sprawled in front.

She slipped onto the sofa.

"I'm sorry Buffie gave you the impression we had something going. We don't and never have. Never will. I've talked to her and told her as much, diplomatically. Her parents were friends of my grandparents in Atlanta. I'm not into social standings. Buffie is. She had a high falutin' husband who died about six years ago. I've been polite to her, but I've never asked her for a date."

"Then what did she mean last night about you coming over to her house?"

"She'd asked me to fix her plumbing. A faucet in her kitchen. I sent my son William."

"Really?"

"Sure. She's not my type. I don't care how much money someone has or who their first cousin once removed is. If you'll let me, I'll show you what I do like...because I like you. I more than like you." His eyes sparkled like a teenage boy, and with his hair rumpled, he appeared years younger and irresistibly manly.

"I'm really not interested in dating. I want to be independent...to be a career woman at last. I'm pursuing Interior Design."

"I respect your plans and I'd like to be a part of them. I have some plans too."

"Well, we can certainly be friends." Her palms went from damp to squishy wet.

"My plans include being more than pals."

"Now Jake, you don't even know me." Her whole body became mush, and her insides shook. Did her voice crack?

"I know enough. Do you believe in love at first sight?"

"No." Not until lately.

"Well, I do. I knew you were the one for me

when you dropped into my arms. I guess you could say when you *fell* for me, I *fell* for you." A grin crawled across his face

He lowered himself to the floor.

Did he see dust bunnies? Why hadn't she polished the hardwoods? What was he doing? Wow, he must have great patellas. He didn't show any sign of pain as he plopped himself down on those sixty-something-year-old knee caps.

He propped himself on one knee. This had all the earmarks of...oh, no. She squirmed on the couch. He wouldn't. She still wore the jeans she'd had on all day and her tee shirt smudged with ketchup. Not that she wanted what he seemed to be aiming for, but she should be dressed for the occasion. The moment wasn't right. She wasn't ready. Stop!

Jake reached for her hand. "Will you...." He cleared his throat, and his voice squeaked. "Will you...."

"Jake, no, wait." She couldn't let this happen.

"Will you marry me?"

Kneeling in front of her, Jake's infectious grin enveloped her heart. Did she hear him clearly? Her hearing had been playing tricks on her.

"Will you do me the honor of becoming my wife?" His eyes melted her.

"Marry you? Be your wife? No. I mean I can't."

"Why not?"

"Well, I don't know you."

"Sure you do. I'm Jake Stewart, cowboy, a guy

who likes to count things, and the man who's madly in love with you." His words warmed her like a dazzling fire on a snowy night. In fact heat and cold rushed through her at the same time. Not even Ansey had ever caused such extremes. Don't think that. She loved Ansey. Could she spend her life with someone who kept her on a roller coaster of emotions?

Excitement chiseled at her fatigue and replaced her unknown future with hope and thoughts of fun. What should she do? Get up? Run? Stay put? Scream? She rose to her bare feet.

Jake followed. His eyes sent electricity pulsing up and down her spine.

Her knees locked, and she teetered.

He cupped her face in his hands and drew her closer. He tapped her lips with his, pulled away, smiled into her eyes, then slid his hands down to her waist. Then he pressed his lips on hers with gentle firmness dissolving her into a romantic fantasy that sent her whirling. She fit perfectly in his arms and against his chest. Could heaven be any better? She wanted to stay there forever. His touch, his cologne, his muscular build all merged to create this ideal man.

But how could she allow such thoughts? She loved Ansey. Guilt swept over her, followed by embarrassment and excitement. Her thoughts fragmented into unintelligible pieces like a jigsaw puzzle that refused to create a picture.

"Angie? Angie?" A voice from a faroff place

called her back to her living room. Jake's gaze held onto her, his timbre melodic. He spoke her name in a way that brimmed with affection. Could that be love? He said her name the way a man says his sweetheart's name.

"Will you, Angie? Will you marry me? Say yes now, and we can elope."

"I shouldn't. No, I can't. Jake, I hardly know you. I still feel married to Ansey." Why did she keep reminding herself about loving Ansey?

"Sophie and Ansey want us to be happy. I bet they're up in heaven playing tennis together and wishing us well. They adore us."

Ansey hated tennis. Maybe they're playing golf though.

"Maybe we should date." Angie stepped back from Jake's lofty figure. She wobbled against the sofa's round arm.

"Okay, let's date for a month. Go out with me tomorrow night. We'll have dinner on the Square and go to whatever play is at the Performing Arts Center. I'll pick you up at six sharp." He stepped closer again.

She strode to the window, then swiveled to face him.

"We can go out tomorrow night, but when I said we should date, I meant date other people too."

"You're wasting your time dating other men. I know."

"How do you know?"

"I've been around. Here's the deal. Eight of the guys you'll meet, you'll never want to see again. Two will want you to be friends, two will want a nurse, and four will want your purse. One will be a liar. Then there's me. Marry me now, so I can save you from the nightmare." That wry grin squiggled across his face again.

Caught between laughing and crying, she stared. Jake thought he was right all of the time.

"I've only been out a couple of times since Ansey died."

"And what was that like?"

"Okay, I guess." She didn't tell him one man whined and talked about himself all night, and the other mumbled and stared at his shoes. That must be *two* off the list of *never wanting to see again.* Won't mention them. Might give him more ammunition for his *don't waste your time dating other men* saga.

"Have your dates like your ice cream flavor of the week—a different man every seven days. Except for me. I get at least two times a week." Jake dipped into the candy dish on the end table and popped a piece of chocolate into his mouth.

"What makes you so special?" She smiled to take the edge off her words.

"I've already declared my love for you, and I'm going to marry you."

"You sound pretty positive."

"My attitude may not solve all my problems but it annoys enough people to make it worth the effort."

He made her laugh. She should lock onto that positive attitude too. His way of thinking could be contagious.

He caressed her hand and grinned. "I'm warning you: I get what I want. I'm persistent and patient." The gleam in his eyes lit a fire in her heart that sent flames swirling through her chest and down her legs, leaving her weak and warm.

"Patient? You gave me a month and told me to make a list."

"I said I'd stay five minutes. It's been an hour, and I'm still here."

She glanced at the antique clock on the fireplace mantel. He was right. Seven o'clock, and she no longer had hunger pangs or fatigue.

"Yeah, at the top of that list, write tall, dark bean counter." He winked.

"I'll put that at number five." She pretended to scrawl something on her hand.

He kissed her like a man in love. "Does that let you know I'm only interested in you?"

"I think we should date others."

"You want me to call Buffie?"

Her body went cold. Not really. She didn't want *him* to date. She wanted to date other men while he pined away at home. That seemed fair. He didn't have to be so confident. Was that egotism or determination?

"You do what you want." She couldn't look him in the eyes.

"Okay, I'll call her."

"You said you weren't interested in Miss Delilah Debutante." Blood rushed to her face and her cheeks burned. Had he noticed?

He started for the door. "Okay, I'll let you prove my point about the men you'll meet. I'll wait at home."

"No, really, you go out all you want." She crossed her fingers behind her back.

"I will. I'll date you twice a week, unless you want to go more." Jake slid his hand around her waist and pulled her to his chest.

She exhaled. "I have a date next Thursday night. A friend of Dixie-Lee's."

He bent to kiss her again, and like an involuntary impulse, she reached up to her highest tiptoes and clasped her hands around his neck. His lips pressed against hers harder this time. Goose bumps budded on her arms.

Did she have to go out with Dixie-Lee's friend?

Chapter 9

Angie glanced at her watch. Five o'clock. Les Boiles had chosen this upscale restaurant for their date. Where was he? Pretty nervy telling her to meet him. Well, maybe not. She'd have her own getaway car if the date warranted a quick exit.

Angie folded her napkin for the sixteenth time. A large man waddled in her direction, peering this way and that. Reminded her of that gray-haired actor S.Z. "Cuddles" Sakall who played in the old, old movie *In the Good Old Summertime* with Judy Garland and Van Johnson. But he didn't seem cuddly like Sakall, and *Les* was definitely *more*, perhaps three hundred pounds *of more.*

He plopped down barely making eye contact and waved to the waiter. "A glass of Chardonnay." He peered over his shoulder, then at Angie. "I guess you must be Angela Crutcher?" His gaze scanned the room like a detective on an obvious case.

"It's Angie, please. Angie Cooper." She

followed his darting glances. "Is everything all right? Did you lose something...or someone?"

"I'm a psychiatrist, and if I run into a patient, they get nervous." He fidgeted.

He's the one who appeared nervous. "We'll do our best to keep this visit between the two of us." She looked to and fro, but no one returned her glances.

Doctor Les is more's eyes kept darting.

"I'm not social, but I've been at this dating game for a while. Not much to it. We'll just eat and visit an hour, then I'll go. Unless you want dessert. Then we'll stay another fifteen minutes."

"Oh." She promised to get Dixie-Lee for this.

"Yeah. I'm Lester Franklin Boiles, sixty-five, been married three times, have no children, don't like sports, dancing, or small talk. I read a lot, mostly journals." He looked up as the waiter set his wine on the table.

Well, that was a clear presentation of the goods.

How fast could she start the motor of her getaway car? Right you are, Jake. Les rated number three on the *hope I never see him again* list.

The waiter paused and sighed before taking their order, then whisked away.

Was their server bored too?

"Do you have hobbies, Doctor Boiles?"

"Not really." He fiddled with his phone.

"Pets?"

"Allergic."

"Favorite dessert?"

"Any flavor of ice cream."

Well, he wouldn't be on her flavor of the week. Was he ever going to ask her anything or acknowledge her presence in some way?

She perused the room like her surroundings might ignite some idea in her head. The waterfall outside provided a soothing backdrop to this night of disappointment. Her head pounded and fiery darts pierced her temples. Could psychiatrists prescribe pain medicine?

They ate in silence, except for an occasional acknowledgement about the food. Her trout had the perfect blend of spices and was browned to her liking. "My baked potato is scrumptious."

"Mine's a little undercooked, and so is the broccoli." Les still consumed his food with ferocity.

"Do you like jokes?"

"Don't know any." His face stayed pointed at his food.

Had he heard the one, *You've brought religion into my life. Now I believe in hell*? Better not mention that one. "Aaa, how about, never go to a doctor...whose office plants have died." Angie giggled into her napkin.

Doctor Boiles' gaze remained fixated on his semi-raw food. "Want dessert?"

"I don't believe so. Thank you for the evening."

"Likewise. Amanda, I'll call you in a couple of weeks."

"Actually, it's Angie." This night was about as

much fun as prickly heat sprouting on her neck.

"Okay. Your share will be $41.75 with tax and tip. I tip big." He slipped his wallet out from inside his coat.

Whoa. Was this the new dating game? She rummaged through her purse and found some mad money in her wallet. She left cash on the table and skedaddled. Was Jake always going to be right?

***

Angie stretched out on her living room sofa and placed a cold cloth on her throbbing head. What a night.

The doorbell chimed an insistent but friendly announcement. Piper had gone to visit her parents in California for a week, and Dixie-Lee had her quilting bee tonight. She would ignore the bell.

The ringing became persistent and irritating. Oh, dear.

She scrambled to the door, flicked on the porch light, and peered through the peep hole.

She tossed the cloth behind a standing potted plant, ruffled her hair, and opened the door.

"Just thought I'd drop by on my way home." Jake handed her two dozen double delight roses and a wide grin.

"Thank you." How did he know those flowers were her favorites? How did he know she'd be home? It was only 6:30. She was sure he'd remembered she'd had a date.

"May I take you out for coffee or iced tea?" Jake had the look of a quarterback who knew which play to call next.

"No, thank you. I was just about to whip up a casserole for tomorrow."

"A casserole at this hour?"

"Our book club, *The Bookies*, learned of a young mom expecting baby number four, who's been commanded to bed rest. Some of us are providing meals to relieve the family of living on hot dogs and macaroni and cheese."

"*The Bookies*?" Jake sported that infectious grin and glint in his eyes.

"We thought a double entendre would be fun. You're welcome to stay if you wouldn't be too bored." She put the flowers in a vase and pulled the ingredients out for the meal prep.

"I can help. I mix up a mean casserole. What kind are you fixin'?"

"Chicken spaghetti."

"My specialty. Hey, how did your date go tonight?"

So he did remember. "Oh, fine." She hoped her nose wasn't growing.

"Are y'all going out again?"

"He said he'd call." She choked on those words.

She glimpsed Jake and giggled all over the pasta.

"What? Which one was he? The never again, liar, wants a nurse, or needs a purse?"

He was so infuriatingly right. Why did he have to be so good looking, and how did he always make her laugh?

Jake gave Angie feelings of safety, security, and contentment. She hated that.

"I had a call from another man, Big John. Going out next week."

"Big John? That's a selfie of a small psyche. Disaster's screaming at you."

Angie held her chuckles inside.

Jake whisked her into his arms and kissed her. Her body tingled from her cerebellum to lower phalanges. He made every fiber of her being come alive and shout for joy.

Could Big John compete with him?

Would Ansey mind?

Why would anyone want to be an independent woman? But she had to stick to her guns. She had to experience fulfillment through work, stand on her own two feet, like all mature people did, and she'd missed. A career would definitely fill the hole in her heart, right? Right.

Chapter 10

Angie crunched down on her Salad Sampler at the Hugs and Quiches Tea Room. She scanned the slice of the antique mall she could see from her seat across from Dixie-Lee. Delicious food and surrounded by bling. The perfect atmosphere for their girls' lunch. Dishes and classic jewelry like her grandmother's shone atop antique furniture, and vintage clothes hung in a far corner.

"Catch me up on things." Dixie-Lee yummed between bites.

"I've actually been pretty busy...dating." Angie dropped her fork and leaned toward Dixie-Lee.

"What? You're keeping secrets from me again."

"I'm telling you now, and you've been either busy or gone." She slathered butter and jam on her warmed scone.

"How did it go with that Doctor Broiler Oven I set you up with?" Dixie-Lee poofed her hair.

"Doctor Les Boiles? I shouldn't even be

speaking to you. He's got the personality of a beach ball...without the fun. How dare you!"

"I'm sorry. Bill thought you'd like him. I shouldn't have entrusted my husband with something as important as romance."

"Then there was this gargantuan man who took me bowling."

"Sounds fun."

"I made a strike for the other team, and my date imploded. My dating's been as excruciating as this Texas heat. I've had my first migraine and had to buy a new ice pack. The latest was Mr. Macho Gym Teacher, and then there was this other guy who was all hands and used language so filthy I had to ask a sailor what two words meant. I only lasted an hour with him. This idea of dating other men might send me smack dab to the macadamia ranch, Jake's euphemism for nut house."

"Darlin', I'm truly sorry. I never dreamed all of this would happen. What about that dreamboat Jake?" Dixie-Lee's eyes sparkled.

"He proposed."

"WHAT? When's the big day?" Her friend screamed so loud half the ladies in the restaurant jumped, a dish toppled over, and two china cups wobbled.

Would the management make them leave? Not to mention breaking things due to high frequency squeals?

"Of course I said no."

Dixie-Lee did a double take. "Why?"

"I barely know Jake, and I want to be an independent business woman, not a married lady accounting to my husband for my every move."

"Now, was it like that to be married to Ansey?"

"No, but I still want independence."

"Darlin', I've had independence, and I know other women who've had it, and we all agree, it's not all tulips and tinsel. A man to love you and share your life with is worth far more than a paycheck and a certificate on a wall. Some women aren't made for marriage, and that's great for them, but that independence mumbo-jumbo isn't for you."

"I hardly know him."

"I know he makes your heart go pit-a-pat, and you think about him all day long, every day." Dixie-Lee stiffened her back against her chair.

"I do not." She did, but how did Dixie-Lee know? "I told him we should date others, and I'm taking design classes." Angie shoved her plate away.

"Foolish girl." Dixie-Lee's eyes brightened like someone who'd just come up with a scientific formula to save mankind. "So, you want him to date that hussy he had falling all over him after Piper's engagement party? Besides other women everywhere, desperate women, in all shapes and voluptuous sizes?"

She squirmed and gulped. "If he wants to." She glanced at her friend. "Well, no. Not really. He said he wasn't going to date anyone except me."

"Oh, so you're going to go out with every Tom, Dick, and Frederick while he waits at home for you. Now, Angie, my darlin', that doesn't sound like you."

"Well, it is me. He said he didn't want to date anyone else. He made that decision, not me. I need some time. He was arrogant enough to even give me a list of the kinds of men I'd find, and offered to marry me on the spot to save me from that misery."

"What kind of list?"

"Oh, he said most men I'd meet I'd never want to see again. Some would be just friends, one would be a liar, some would need a nurse, and others would want my money, what little I have."

"And how's Jake's list workin' so far?" Dixie-Lee added lemon to her hot tea.

She dropped her napkin on her empty plate. "I've got five on my never want to see again list, none on the friends list, one liar, and zero on my may want to consider list."

"You have one on your *betcha want to consider docket*. Jake. Jake's out-of-this-world-gorgeous, and from what I've heard a great all-around-guy. Three-fourths of the single women over fifty from McKinney to Dallas are asking God every night for him to light their candles. When do you see him again?"

"Tomorrow. It was his idea to take dancing lessons. We'll have an early dinner, take the lessons, and afterwards the studio is having a dance for all the students."

"Dinner and a dance? And you aren't ready to snatch this guy up and hold on for dear life? He could get away, ya know. How would you feel if he did?"

Her pulse raced but her body froze. How long would Jake wait for her? Was she playing with fire? Was she playing with a man's heart? How could a woman her age be so mixed up? Was she inconsiderate and selfish—or just scared?

Chapter 11

Happiness cartwheeled inside Angie as she took Jake's hand. He had that affect on her. He clasped her waist and swung her over a mud puddle, muscles flexing under his sleeves, and his jaw pulsing that masculine twitch.

A boom bounced in her heart so hard surely Jake heard it, but he didn't even blink.

With her arm in his, they entered the restaurant through double glass doors. Crisp white tablecloths, water goblets, blue hydrangeas in round vases, and ornate silverware brandished their elegance. Soft violin music floated through the air. As Angie slid into her seat, Jake reached for her hand. Her heart fluttered. His touch and mischievous glint always provoked a ripple and a quiver. A grown woman succumbing to self-consciousness from a simple glance was crazy, right?

"I'm going bowling Tuesday night. Would you like to go?" Jake leaned toward her.

Her body froze. After the fiasco with Big John, she never wanted to see another bowling ball. "I'm not very good at that. Maybe we can do something else."

"I understand. Not important."

He didn't care if she couldn't bowl. She could breathe again.

"What about golf?"

"Don't know how but might be willing to learn." She reached for a roll and butter.

"I'm not very good at dancing, but I'm looking forward to trying a few steps. Hope you don't mind if I stumble around the floor." He searched her face.

Did he need her approval to be a bad dancer? "I'm sure you'll be fine. I love dancing, but I'm far from being a pro." She finished her popover. A piece of heaven.

***

The glossy dance floor stretched out in front of Angie, lights bright. About six couples bristled and laughed. Were they nervous too?

The lessons began right on time. Oh, dear.

"Hi, everyone. I'm Mitch and this is Madge, your dance instructors tonight." Both thin as twigs, they bowed and smiled. "We'll start with the Foxtrot. Gentlemen, you'll begin with your left foot."

"Which one?" Jake stared at the floor and stuck out a foot.

"Your other left." Mitch grinned.

Jake thudded to the other foot.

"Watch carefully." Mitch and Madge moved with skilled deliberation. "It's slow, slow, quick, quick. Slow, slow, quick, quick...to form a box." They sailed around the floor, holding their bodies straight in graceful parallel moves.

Madge's chiffon dress swirling above slender ankles and her feet gliding to the music struck a responsive nerve. Angie glanced at her knee-length skirt and low heels. Not as glamorous, but safer. She would've tripped in a long dress and fallen off stilettos.

"Your turn." Mitch motioned, and Madge arched her back. "Follow us, everybody."

Jake shook his legs like he was getting the kinks out.

Angie braced herself.

Shoes squeaked, breaths swooshed, and would-be *Freds and Gingers* clasped arms.

"Step, step, side together. Back, back, side close." Mitch and Madge smiled as they sailed around the floor.

"This is going to be easy." Angie puffed out some air. But her feet locked, then tangled together. Jake caught her. What must he think? She wasn't clumsy. Except with him.

"We can do this. How hard can it be?" Jake drew her close.

They rambled together in a small space, then took off. Shooting along the shiny, mahogany floor and bumping into other dance students, they pounded on.

She and Jake stopped with a jolt. Whew!

"Now for more fun and style, add step, step, side close, rise and *fall*." Mitch belted out.

Angie grinned at Jake.

"Now with music." The teachers stepped to the beat.

Jake nodded and tossed her *that look* that made her dissolve. He took off in smooth strides with her hanging on. This hunk of brawniness proved to be light on his feet, those size fourteens moving with ease. His warmth felt delicious against her back and on her hands.

Strains of music filled the ballroom.

Jake gave her a glance like her favorite emoticon on her cell phone.

His hands radiated security that sent giggles permeating her body and soul. He gave her life, fun-filled, hopeful, and energetic.

She could dance in Jake's arms forever. She wouldn't need an ice pack tonight.

Her feet didn't touch the ground as she drifted to the car holding Jake's hand, while silvery moonbeams lit their path.

Angie smiled inside, listening to the sounds of nighttime.

Jake took the long way to her house, winding through tree-lined avenues with old fashioned street lights casting pearly glows on the houses and lawns.

He swung into her driveway.

"Like to come in for coffee?" She didn't want the evening to end.

He walked her to the door and dropped onto her swing. He drew her into the crook of his shoulder.

She nestled there as content as she'd ever been in her life.

"Angie, you know I love you. Ready to marry me?" The porch light gave him a heavenly radiance.

"Oh, Jake, I have to admit I had a wonderful night with you. Every time I spend with you is fabulous...but...."

"But, what?" Jake cupped her chin and peered into her eyes.

He ignited a flame in her that made her dizzy and her arms and legs limp. Was she responding to his animal magnetism or having a heart attack? Could he be good for her health?

"Darling..." Jake kissed her.

When she came up for air, she wiggled to one side. "After Piper and Brad get married, I'm going to pursue a career. Never really had one. I'm taking design courses. I want to be on my own. Pictures of colorful swatches reel through my constant thoughts. I'm showing some chintz to some clients next week." Was hurt brewing in his eyes?

"You can have anything you desire if you marry me. I want you to be happy. Independence doesn't mean you have to be alone. Go to school, work with your fabrics, just do it from my house with me."

Her heart fluttered as fast as a hummingbird gulping espresso. "I'm not sure I want to be married. Marriage is difficult. My life is on an even keel. Peaceful. Matrimony, though wonderful, involves upheaval and arguments, in the best circumstances."

"What squabbles? With grown children, we'll have no child-rearing issues. I have a nest egg so no money problems, and I'll support your career. We're more mature than the first time, and we know how to love better. Smooth sailing if you ask me."

How to *love better*? She thought of him far more than she thought of herself, and that warmed her heart. She was ready to love him the way he needed to be loved. He needed time and affection, and she thrilled in giving both. With Ansey she'd thought of herself more. Sorrow invaded her heart. If only she could apologize to that dear man. She longed to scream *yes, now*, to Jake, but the words lodged in her throat.

"Please give me more time. I'll make a decision soon."

"Promise?"

"Yes."

"I'll wait...as long as the answer is yes." Jake pressed his lips against hers, then released her. He brushed her hair back. "Hurry. I can't sweat bullets too long."

What did he mean by that, and why couldn't she tell him she loved him?

Chapter 12

"Hello, Dixie-Lee. I could tell by the excited jangle it was you." Angie removed one earring while finagling the receiver and placed her earring on the bedside table.

"So glad my personality reaches through phone lines. Hey, where have you been, girlfriend? I've been dragging the river for you."

"I was on a date. Remember Chuck Broadwater from high school?" She removed the other earring.

"Who?" Dixie-Lee's voice dropped in pitch.

"You know, valedictorian, president of the Latin and Chemistry Clubs, guy voted Most Likely to Succeed. The one all the girls wanted to date. Well, he just blew into town and asked me out. His wife died a year ago, and he was in town for a convention."

"Can't place him, and why did you go out with him when you have perfect-mate-Jake pantin' after you?"

"Well, Chuck remembers you big-time."

"Really. I guess he's sorta smart then." Her smile pranced through the airwaves.

"Hold on." Angie dropped the phone and slid out of her clothes. She slipped her nightgown over her head. "I'm back. And, he took me to the Mansion in Turtle Creek."

"Swanky, huh?"

"Chuck's a lawyer, has a daughter at USC, and owns two houses, one in Beverly Hills and one in Manhattan."

"So he's got hot and cold runnin' money?"

"You know I don't care about big bucks. He's a nice guy, impeccable manners. Seemed a little sad though."

"What does he look like?"

"He's fine. Blond hair has turned silver, and he still wears horn-rimmed glasses."

"Just fine, huh, as in C-minus?"

"Okay, he's very nice." Irritation poked at Angie.

"Are you saying you're interested?"

"I'm not saying anything. Just stating facts." Angie plopped on her bed.

"Don't wait too long. Now, darlin', remember what I told you about the age thing."

"What thing? You have a rule for everything."

"You know. The woman needs to be younger than the man she marries, but at a certain age, that gets harder, maybe impossible."

"Well, at that certain age, whatever that is, age

doesn't matter." Throbbing attacked Angie's temples.

"Yes, it does matter. A man wants a younger woman. Mark my words. Even Cleo Mae, eighty-seven got hitched to Walter Ambrose, who was ninety-one. We know Chuck is our age since he was in our class, but how old is Jake?"

"It really doesn't matter because I'm not going to marry Chuck or Jake or anybody else." Should she tell Dixie-Lee that Chuck had bragged about skipping a grade and having a December birthday? He was almost two years younger than they were.

"How is the list workin' for ya?" Dixie-Lee's voice raised an octave.

"Oh, yeah. Well, Chuck could be a definite maybe. If I decide to marry." Angie coughed. She always coughed when she stretched the truth.

"Don't scratch Jake off your list yet. Check out this guy Chucky Broadstream before you buy a white dress and throw posies."

"Broad-water. Dixie-Lee, really. I'm just saying Chuck is a nice guy, and it might be fun to date someone from high school. And his having some money only adds mystery."

Angie couldn't stifle the yawn or the squeak that followed.

"Okay, girlfriend, I can take a hint. Talk to you in the morning. Sweet dreams...about Jake."

***

A thunderous blast bolted Angie out of a deep sleep. She scrambled for the clock. Two fifteen.

Zsa Zsa hopped off the bed and raced in circles, yapping her shrillest yelps.

"Zsa Zsa, please" She grabbed her nervous dog and cradled her with soft shushing.

Where was the phone? She patted the bed clothes and under her pillow. Oh, goodness, that middle of the night call everyone dreads. Her mind darted from one family member to another—Piper was in California with her parents, so they wouldn't be calling. Her sons? Oh, dear, where was the phone? Her grandchildren? Her heart beat out of her chest. Finally she found the contraption under a blanket. Her hands sweated.

"He...llo?"

A man's voice. Vaguely familiar.

"Who? What? Who is this?"

"Angie, wake up. This is Chuck Broadwater, your school chum. Honey, you won't believe this. Of all things. There's been a terrible mistake."

"What? What mistake?"

"Angie, dear. I'm in jail and need bail. I need you to bring me ten thousand dollars by eight this morning."

Heavens to Betsy. Where was that list? Chuck catapulted to first place on *never want to see again!*

Chapter 13

Angie fluffed her hair and curbed a giggle. "Thank you, Jake, for an out-of-this-world fantastic day at the Arboretum." Visions of gorgeous purple snapdragons, sunflowers, asters, and pansies danced in her head. Sunshine whispered love songs, and cooling breezes tousled her hair. One outstanding day of whim and whimsy.

"Where are we going Saturday?" Jake pulled her close and wrapped his arms around her waist. How perfectly she fit into his hug.

"I'm committed to a program for the Dallas Theological Seminary Wives. Some of us baby-sit to give the moms a chance to hear lectures, eat a meal they didn't prepare, and relax and visit with other adults."

"May I go too?" Jake gave her that wide-eyed glint she loved.

"Sure, I suppose. It'll be three hours of non-stop little ones. I'll call the lady in charge and get you a background check."

"I'm up for the job, ma'am." He saluted.

***

Angie let the night caress her senses. Stars twinkled in the ebony sky. Jake swaddled his strong arms around her under the light on the front porch. He bent to kiss her. Electrical currents shot through her. A day with high-spirited children, a beautiful dinner at her favorite restaurant, a stroll around nearby shops, and more getting-to-know-you time with Jake. He confessed to being a sports fanatic, especially loving baseball and football, and she admitted she called grandchildren when she got in a bind with a computer or cell phone.

"Jake, thank you for a superlative day, flawless in every way. I so enjoyed the children at the seminary."

"Me, too. Especially when you told them about Adam and Eve."

"You mean when the leaf floated down from the book, and the little girl piped up with, 'Miss Cooper, I think this is Adam's suit.'" Angie's heart smiled.

"And, those tykes moved faster than ants on a snickerdoodle. Whew!" Jake beamed. "Want to make the day more perfect?" He stroked her hair out of her face.

"Well, sure, but the day already was."

"Then say you'll marry me." His warm breath breathed happiness into her soul.

The enormous moon shone bright, bathing everything in fairy-tale radiance. Jake leaned toward her like a benevolent giant. Sparks ricocheted up and down her spine. Blooming roses swirled fragrance around her head.

"I'm *in love* with you, Angie, darling. Will you marry me?"

"Jake, I'm ready to give you my answer."

He lifted her chin. "If it's a yes, answer. If not, silence is golden."

Was Jake stammering?

"I can't believe I'm gonna say this." Angie searched Jake's eyes.

His facial expression fell hard and fast. "If it's bad, don't say anything."

"I think you'll approve." She held her breath.

Jake didn't move a muscle.

"I love you too." Firecrackers burst from her heart. From somewhere music played. Was that melody from another house or from her soul enraptured in tonight's events? Could he see her heart palpitating into her throat?

"You do? You love me?" Jake's eyes shone.

"Yes, and I want to marry you." The words lit her up from head to toe.

"Yahoo, and praise the Lord!" He grabbed her and swung her around and around.

She giggled and spun.

He set her down, framed his warm masculine hands on her face, and kissed her like a cherished woman.

The night reeled. Was it from excitement, love, or the spinning?

She'd never been so sure of anything. She had wanted to marry Jake from the first moment she'd seen him, but guilt that somehow she'd be rejecting Ansey had created a boulder of despair. Fear she couldn't be happy twice in her life paralyzed her, and slicing pain resulting from the rejection by both her biological and adoptive fathers robbed her of peace and confidence. But she remembered her pastor's advice not to let grief or unwarranted guilt seep into her soul and take residence there. If Jake was a good man and she loved him, which he was and she did, and if she prayed and had peace with her decision, then she should go forward with her life. Her pastor's words erased doubt and guilt and showered her with calm.

And, then the burgeoning desire for independence and a career. She'd secretly envied women who'd thrived in professions while keeping the home fires burning. Always wanted a taste of that existence. But could it be that she'd had what she needed all along? Marriage with devotion and passion. And she could have that life again, plus a career, encouraged by Jake. Stop, your shaking legs. Be strong. Be young. Be happy.

***

Were Jake's ears playing tricks on him? Angie had said yes. His prayers had been answered. Were those stars above Angie's house brighter than before? The streetlights flickered their approval.

Happiness chased him like a bloodhound on a

scent. He would do everything in his power to make her happy. *Thank You, Lord, for giving me the desire of my heart—a loving bride who not only loves You, but me too. I had prayed for a wife, but didn't ask for a beautiful one. Well, maybe I did mention looks once or twice. With Angie You answered a favorite scripture from Ephesians 3:20: Now all glory to God, who is able, through His mighty power at work within us, to accomplish infinitely more than we might ask or think. You did that, Lord.*

Standing on her front porch, he smiled. "How soon can we get hitched? I'm ready now, but I know you women need time to do whatever it is you do. Whatever you want is what I want. Just soon though. I'm not getting any younger."

With moonbeams dazzling her hair and face, Angie glowed. Maybe these thoughts were extreme, but this night provoked extremes. His face hurt from smiling, but he'd grin all the way to their wedding day and beyond.

"Angie, honey, let's shout our love from the rooftops! Let's set the date! Would tomorrow be too soon?" He tilted off the front step, but caught himself. He jumped back up on the porch, bent down, and embraced her.

***

Angie's heart beat so hard and so fast she could count the beats. Would the staccato slow down? Would Jake stop bouncing? Was he in his right mind? Did he know what he'd asked? What she'd answered? He was absolutely manic.

Jake took her in his arms and swirled her through the yard. "Let's dance all night, and get married in the morning."

"Tomorrow is a bit too soon. We have to tell our families." Could she be ready in a month?

He stopped twirling and blew out several breaths. "I know. I'll invite everyone to my house. We'll have a barbeque and spring the good news on them. I'll have Tillie Mae get the house ship-shape, and I'll call a caterer."

"Okay. Can we round up our families in a week?" Her words fell out in breathless spurts.

"We'll do it." Typical Jake—assurance.

"I won't be able to sleep a wink, but we have to get some rest, so you'd better skedaddle." A smile wiggled from her toes and squeezed out.

"You're telling me to go home? Already? It's early. Only midnight."

"That's early?" Was this man crazy? Could she keep up with this guy? She wasn't the least bit tired either. She couldn't stop giggling. Did she look like a woman in love?

***

A zillion details for a gargantuan family gathering shook Angie's brain. She didn't dare talk to Dixie-Lee. Her friend would finagle out every tidbit of news. Angie called her daughter in California to set up face time with her and her family. Just didn't mention she'd be calling from Jake's house, a house she'd never seen—ever.

Hallelujah, Piper and Brad had a free night and would be there. In fact, everyone invited could come. Perfection applauded their plans. Nothing could go wrong now.

Chapter 14

Angie's palms sweated, and her head throbbed. The fateful night had arrived later than planned but still came too soon. Breezes whispered through a thousand trees on Jake's property. Outdoor lights and stars blinked lighthearted favor. All things percolated along as planned.

She sauntered through Jake's one-story home that covered half the state of Texas, eyeing oversized furniture and giant pictures on the walls. Her thoughts raced to how she could make changes to this masculine décor, with Jake's approval of course. Giant pictures of family and others of horses filled the walls. Scraped mahogany-colored floors and chocolate-colored walls in the entrance and den greeted her, and a standing portrait of Sophie loomed over a rugged stone fireplace. Was he having trouble letting go? She swallowed hard and hurried outside.

Jake patted his hyper dog. "Angie meet Bob."

"Bob?"

"Yeah, I've had my hairy friend since he was a pup." Jake turned. "Hey, Bob, go get Heather."

"Your dog is Bob? Who's Heather?"

"The cat." Jake grinned that mischievous grin of his, then waltzed from one knot of people to another. She followed. Hard to stifle the giggles. Giddiness mounted and could get the best of her, but all in a night's work.

Angie heaved in a big breath, pressed down her skirt with dewy hands. A thousand volts of excitement shot throughout her body. One more stimuli and she'd go up in flames. Both clans full of barbequed brisket, potato salad, green bean casserole, corn-on-the-cob, and assorted desserts, quipped and cut up. Jake fashioned the outdoor wide screen TV for FaceTime so Susan and her family could join them. Susan shifted on her own sofa beside her husband Bryan, fixing her blue-eyed gaze on the rambunctious backyard group.

Jake waved to the crew on the expansive patio. "Hey, everyone. Hey, ya'll. Thank you for coming and on such short notice."

Applause rose from the families, and she joined in.

"Thank you and love you, Dad and Grandpa," thundered from his tribe.

"Thank you, Mr. Stewart" rang from her kinfolk.

Cheeriness collided with exuberance.

"I have some exciting news to share with all of you. I couldn't wait to tell you."

Angie loved the expression on Jake's face.

"Hurry, Grandpa!" The children's whistles rode the airwaves.

"I have...well, Angie and I, have this wonderful news." He turned to clasp her hand. "Our dear family, we want you to be the first to know that Angie and I have fallen in love and plan to be married."

Gasps drifted through the crowd. Silence.

Her heart fell flat.

Susan's stoic face hung suspended on the huge screen. Were those tears in her eyes? Happy tears wouldn't make her shoulders slump. Bryan stirred beside her without expression.

"Grams." Piper reached for her hand. "Grams, what are you thinking? This is embarrassing."

Julianne pulled her father close, but her high pitch voice carried. "Dad, you're acting like a silly adolescent. Have you already forgotten Mom? I can't believe you're doing this to our family."

Could this cold dismay be happening? Didn't their families wish happiness for their loved ones?

Anger tied to deep hurt tangled in her chest.

Chapter 15

Angie drooped, her spirit still, as Jake drove her home. Ice rained into her every thought. She grabbed a tissue from her purse and tried not to sniffle too loud. The night that had begun with hope, beauty, and excitement plummeted into despair. Even the sky had let her down. Dark clouds rumbled in and drowned her dreams.

Jake walked her to her door without a word. He leaned toward her and wiped tears from her face. "Angie, honey, we'll be all right. Our families are sensible, caring, loving people. They'll come around. We'll give them time, and we'll pray. The Lord has shown us He's on our side." Jake kissed her with a soft brush of his lips.

"I never dreamed our love would create this rift. I'm sorry, Jake, but I can't marry you now."

"Let's talk in the morning. The sun will shed hope on our situation."

***

Tension trampled Angie's days and flooded her

nights into somber weeks. Getting little sleep, her eyes swelled, and her back ached. Late autumn rained gloom.

"Bye, Grams. Be home about eleven." Piper rushed out the front door before Angie could respond. Another night alone.

Angie curled on the sofa in the family room. How could her kith and kin not understand? Would things ever be right between her and the light of her life?

She closed her eyes while thoughts ravaged her mind. Her family surmised Jake only wanted her to take care of him in old age, completely ignoring his current robust health and their closeness in age. His family thought her a fortune hunter and frivolous because she and Jake went out often and she giggled a lot. How much money did he have anyway? He drove a seventeen-year-old car, for Pete's sake. And both families thought she and Jake were too old for dating, love, and remarriage. Oh, the ignorance of youth.

Nestled into her big chair in her bedroom, she scanned her Bible. She stopped at Psalm 18. The words tugged at her heart. Verse 16: *He reached down from heaven and rescued me; He drew me out of the deep waters.* And, then in verse 19: *He led me to a place of safety; He rescued me because He delights in me.*

Please rescue me, Lord. I'm drowning in these deep waters of sadness, and I can't feel Your delight. You know, dear Lord, how difficult it is for me to understand You love me, but I claim these scriptures and plead for You to help me accept Your will. In Jesus' name. Amen.

The door bell chimed.

She ran to the restroom and splashed water on her face. She peeked through the peep hole. Todd. What was her son doing here?

She flung open the door.

"Hi, Mom. I brought us some Chinese food. You still like it, don't cha?"

An anemic smile attempted to show itself as she ambled to the kitchen/den. "Yes, thank you. I didn't know you were coming. Is the family with you?"

"It's just me. A last minute decision." He handed her chopsticks. "Let's talk."

Zsa Zsa scampered between Todd's feet, and then tucked herself into her dog bed.

"I'm not sure I want to. What do you want to talk about?" She breathed hard.

"You and Mr. Stewart. I'm trying to understand." Todd dropped the bags of food on the table.

"Thank you. I appreciate that." She patted Todd's arm.

"It's only been a few years since Dad died. Wasn't he as great a husband as he was a father?" Her son's stare bore into her, slowing her heartbeat.

"Todd! You know he was. I still love him. Yes, your father was a tremendous man, as terrific as you, but Jake is a wonderful man, too, who's filled an ache in my heart. He understands that I still love your father and always will. He loves his deceased wife. But, the sad truth is our spouses died, and we're still alive...and alone."

"Is finding another husband so important? You're so busy with Piper, your friends, and church work. How can you be lonely?"

"Well, I can be and I am." How could a grown man be so dense? "But I fell in love too."

"Have you considered if Jake becomes your husband, he may be the only grandfather my children remember? That stranger will be Grandpa. That dishonors Dad and cuts me deep in my gut."

"I wish your father hadn't died. You should know that. Share your good memories of Dad. We'll encourage those recollections. His blood runs through their veins. Some children don't know any grandparents. Jake will love your children, and I will love Jake's grandchildren. Find the blessing, not the pain."

"Let's eat before the food gets cold, and we'd better change the subject for our digestion's sake." Todd spread the food out and put place mats on the table.

She retrieved glasses of water.

"Great news. My three preschoolers are hardy, healthy, and wise." Todd beamed from ear to ear. "Billy is on the T-ball All-Stars, Davey learned to write his whole name, and Jana loves her new purple tutu." Todd lit up.

Good to hear some upbeat, everyday conversation. Her heart hadn't allowed fun for a long while.

"The choir is practicing for Christmas, and the homeless shelter is revving up for more people due to the holidays." She picked up their glasses.

"I know you love your choir work, and the homeless have taken residence in your heart." Todd smiled and helped her gather the all too familiar white Chinese take-out boxes.

"Thank you for bringing dinner. Loved the Chinese, especially the egg rolls." A smile didn't fit on her face anymore, but she forced one.

"You're welcome." His kiss warmed her cheek.

"Where are Brittany and the kids?" She crammed leftovers into a box.

"Florida. They're visiting her parents for a month. I thought I'd go crazy if I spent one more night at home alone. The house is so quiet and empty. I'll never tell Brit she can go away again. You can't believe how lonely I am."

"Oh, yes I can. I bet I know exactly how you feel, and *your* family's coming back."

"Touché, Mom." Todd wrapped her in a hug.

Chapter 16

Angie placed her book on the coffee table and stared at the wall in her den.

"I'll be home early tonight. Wanna have dinner together? My treat." Piper's sweet face glowed pink. She hugged Angie on her way out.

Had things changed between them?

Angie answered the phone on the third ring. "Hi, honey. What? Sure you and your family can drop by tomorrow night, but you don't have to bring supper. Oh, okay. Thanks."

Hmm...number two son Eric had a zing in his voice. What's going on? Had Todd had a heart-to-heart with the family?

The phone rang again.

"Hi, Mom. Do you have a minute?"

"Susan! Sure, honey. How's the Golden State?" Was her voice light enough?

"We haven't fallen into the ocean yet, and the weather's still perfect, but that's not why I called."

"Oh? Okay." Perspiration beaded on her

forehead and nose.

"Mom, I am so sorry for my lackluster response to your wedding announcement. I, of all people, should've understood. With Bryan traveling as much as he does, I know about loneliness." Susan sniffled. "He and I talked a lot about your circumstances. Todd called three nights ago, and last night Eric and I talked for four hours. All of us want you to be happy. Will you forgive me?" Sobs swallowed the rest of Susan's words.

Angie's throat tightened. Was it anxiety or gratitude? After almost choking, she stammered, "Of course I forgive you. I love you. Thank you for understanding. And, yes, I've been lonely, but I'm also in love."

"I know, Mom, and I am happy for you. Truly."

Angie laughed and cried through the rest of the conversation.

"Good-bye. I love you," Susan blubbered.

Angie croaked and sniffled. "Good-bye, honey. I love you too."

She leapt at the sound of the ringing doorbell and ran to the kitchen, pulled a dishtowel from the sink and wiped her wet eyes and face.

"Darling. I had to see you." Jake's pale face drooped under his mop of dark hair that squirmed into a mess. And as usual his shoes left muddy prints.

She patted her face. She must look a fright after that emotional talk with Susan. "Are you all right?"

"Not really." Jake started toward the front door. "I thought we'd walk and talk, and if we get hungry, we'll have a bite."

She placed a hand on his arm. "I've got something to tell you." Was that a flutter in her heart? A couple of weeks had passed since she'd had a bounce or flitter.

"Yeah? Better be good." Jake's lips crept to a half grin.

"I've had a visit and two phone calls. My whole family, even the grandchildren, have given me their blessings. Do you still want to marry me?" Her heart tried to smile. Would his?

"You betcha." Color returned to Jake's face.

"Well, if your family accepts the idea, I'm willing and able." She searched his eyes.

"I've been discussing things with them, and I see signs of weakening. Let's set a date." He squeezed her hand.

"We'll wait a little longer. I don't want them to feel ignored or think we don't care about their feelings." She flipped a sweater from a hanger and slung the wrap over her shoulders.

An open wound festering in agony. That's what her life had been. Now possibly only the final remnants of that raw laceration lay between family and happiness.

***

Angie and Jake strolled, her hand safe in his, through a small, manicured park. They spoke in whispers and laughed soft sounds. The purple and pinks lit the sky and pushed the clouds into the night. The stars poked sparkles of hope into the night sky.

"Mark my words, we'll be married by Christmas." A smile simmered on Jake's face.

She loved how he held her close and stroked her hair.

He had that glint in his eyes again.

Chapter 17

Angie mopped the family room, dusted the knickknacks, and fluffed the sofa pillows. Had to stay busy or go crazy. Where was Jake? What was he doing? Hadn't seen hide nor hair of him in three days. She missed that whisper of his deep bass voice. Certainly there was an explanation, but what? No daily checking in with words of encouragement or ideas for their wedding? Had he tired of convincing his family their marriage was the right thing? Oh, she didn't like the stabbing thoughts that his family still didn't want her. Every one of the sixteen members of his rowdy tribe had to come around.

She'd left messages on his landline's voice mail. She'd called his cell phone, but the contraption stopped ringing almost as soon as it started. Was the phone turned off? She'd emailed, but he'd warned he didn't use that much. She'd driven out to his place, but no one was home. If he'd changed his mind, he'd certainly have had the decency to let her know through some form of twenty-first century technology. Or better yet, he'd have come in person.

The phone blasted. Hope soared but fell again when she read the Caller ID. Dixie-Lee. Had better answer. Dixie-Lee would have the police after her if she kept ignoring her calls.

"Hi, Dix. How are you?" Could Dixie-Lee hear anxiety in her voice?

Her pal's words shot like bullets. "It's how you are that matters? Where have you been?"

"Right here. In a nutshell, Jake proposed, I said yes, but both families put the kibosh on the nuptials. Then my darlings came around. Jake told me he might have to leave, but didn't tell me why or where he was going. Now, no one has heard from him." Angie's hands shook and her knees weakened into Jell-O.

"I'll be over in fifteen minutes."

Hearing Dixie-Lee's southern drawl soothed her nerves. She'd missed her and wanted her to come.

***

"Darlin', have you thought of foul play?" Her friend's serious squint gazed through dark eyelashes into a veil of concern.

"You certainly know how to lift my spirits."

"I'm not trying to scare you, just being realistic." She circled Angie's living room, behind the couch and past the end table.

"That gruesome thought has spiked across my

mind, but I can't let fear plant a thorny bush there."

"Have you talked to his children?" Her best bud kept moving as if an unseen force propelled her.

"I told Piper today, and she called Brad. He said Julianne was out of town too, and no one he'd reached had heard a word. Said he'd always contacted them in the past when he traveled."

"A little odd to say the least, but let's notify the police and put in a missing person on him." Dixie-Lee picked up the phone.

"I'm not sure we should do that yet. He told me he'd be gone three or four days."

"Well, I've checked him out."

"What?"

"Don't look so shocked. I don't want you mixed up with someone who's not rowing with both oars. He could be a mass murderer. Bill did the background check for me." Dixie-Lee pivoted around the coffee table.

"You shouldn't have done that, at least without my knowledge or permission." Angie slipped the phone away and hung up the receiver.

"I thought I'd apologize later if you didn't approve. Well, anyway, we got all good news. Jake's completely on the up and up. Did you know that he preaches at his little church in Gunter sometimes and at one in Waxahachie?" Dixie-Lee dropped onto the sofa.

"No, he hadn't told me." Should Angie smile or

weep?

"All this info on this upstanding citizen makes it look like foul play."

***

Angie's eyelids fluttered. Darkness. Jake floated toward her. She reached out but couldn't touch him. He kept drifting. He whispered, *I love you*, but never came close enough for her to touch him.

Jake, where are you? Are you coming home?

He hovered but she couldn't hear his answer over the train's long, harsh whistles and dogs barking. Why wouldn't everything be quiet so she could hear Jake? *Shhhhhh.*

Her eyes burst open. The phone's cacophonous ring startled her. Zsa Zsa yapped in her ear. Had she been dreaming? Seeing Jake had been so real. She glanced at the clock. Two in the morning. The phone clanging in the middle of the night. Not again. Was Chuck Broadwater out of jail and in need of money? She covered her ears. Caller ID read Private Caller. Did she dare answer? More bad news? She couldn't take any more, but the black thingamajig wouldn't stop.

"Hello?" She held her breath.

Static almost drowned the voice on the other end. "Angie, honey, I'm so sorry to call you at this hour, but this was my only chance."

Who was this? "Chuck?"

"Who's Chuck?" The male voice deepened.

"This is Jake, your fiancé? I am still your intended, aren't I?"

"Jake? Jake, is it really you? Where are you? Are you all right? I've been frantic."

"Sure, I'm okay. What do you mean where am I? Didn't Julianne tell you?"

"I'm sorry, Jake, but I never heard from your daughter. I've been looking all over Texas for you." Angie pulled herself to an upright position.

"Well, I'll be taking my daughter to the woodshed. I'm so sorry. I've tied up some loose ends. Right now I'm in Miami. I'll be home soon and I'll tell you everything. I've gotta go now. I love you. I love you. See you tomorrow. I promise."

The silence cut like a knife. She crumbled. Sobs poured out of her body and soul. Zsa Zsa licked her face and whimpered. "Is it going to be okay, Zsa? Do you think it's all going to work out? What's Jake been doing?"

Chapter 18

Angie flung her purse into the living room closet. The sun still slept. She checked the clock on the mantel, six. A lifetime had passed since she'd seen Jake. She peeked out the front window. Lights on houses twinkled like birthday candles, and the pre-dawn blue sky glimmered hope. A shadow moved on the front step. Her heart jumped. She opened the door. "Jake!" She flew into his arms, then reared back.

"I don't know if I should hit you or kiss you!" She rapped his shoulder.

"Definitely kiss me." He leaned in and pressed his lips on hers.

Oh, what a soothing sensation his touch bestowed.

"Oh, honey, I'm so sorry for the mix-up and the anguish I caused. Please forgive me and my temporarily wayward daughter. I'll be talking to Julianne later. Living without you was miserable." He hugged her, then motioned toward the porch swing. "I brought some coffee and doughnuts. Let's watch our first sunrise together while I tell you what I've been up to." His face cracked into a smile.

She scuffled to the den and returned with two lap quilts. She wrapped herself in one, and offered the other to Jake. She slid onto the swing, and swayed with Jake's rhythm. She cocooned into his shoulder. A perfect fit. The cold breeze against the warmth of his skin caressed her senses.

Zsa Zsa curled near her favorite planter.

He sipped some java and cleared his throat.

"Have I told you my father was a POW in WWII?" His eyes grew serious.

"No, you didn't."

"I'll try to condense a long story. He was a Navy man on the USS Houston when the Japanese sank his ship in 1942."

"How terrible."

"Dad had nightmares for the rest of his life."

"I'm so sorry."

"His closest POW buddy, Daniel Everitt Leeson, known as Lee, or *Leethal*, died in 1989, but his wife Mary lived until last week. She needed help with some important papers, and her daughter couldn't get there. Mary knew her health was failing, and I'd promised Dad to help the Leeson family if they ever needed anything. When Mary called, I took the first plane to her home in Miami." He took a bite of donut.

"So that's why you left in such a hurry?" Angie held her cup close and inhaled the heat.

"Yes, and I'd called Julianne when I left at three in the morning, and she vowed to call you."

"I believe she's away right now."

"Where is she?" Jake stiffened.

"Not sure. What did you and Mrs. Leeson talk about?" She set her coffee on a small wicker table.

"The war, Lee, Dad, life." Jake's eyes dimmed. "The survivors became slave labor on the Railway to Death, the rail system from Bangkok to Burma."

She pulled the quilt around her neck and shuddered.

***

"I won't go into detail, but after Dad had endured weeks of torture, Lee secretly shared his meager rations with him. We owed my father's life to Lee."

"An extraordinary debt. I see why you loved Lee and his family. What was your father like after the war?"

"Dad made sure we appreciated God, family, and the United States, no ifs, ands, or buts." Jake straightened. "Since they'd been treated so savagely because of their national heritage, Dad never allowed any semblance of racism. Lee believed the same." Jake rubbed his face.

"You were blessed to have him for a father. Wished I could've met him. How did they get through their tortuous days?" She clutched his arm.

"Dad and Lee shared scripture verses. Others caught on. Helped calm frayed nerves and brought some to a saving knowledge of Jesus Christ." His eyes pierced hers. "Plus, they sang, played harmonicas, put on skits, and even told jokes. These buddies packed away raw memories and recounted jokes the rest of their lives."

"They were strength personified." Love for these unknown men filled her chest.

He nodded. "That's why I vanished." He stroked her hair. "Forgiven?"

"Maybe...this time, but don't ever leave without telling me directly." She hugged him.

Jake held her.

Light snow floated to the ground, and *O Holy Night* from somewhere wafted through the chilled air.

Christmastime, her favorite time of year. She snuggled safe and secure in Jake's embrace. The fragrance of his cologne, the beating of his heart, and his magnetism shot powerful jolts through her body.

He kissed her forehead, her nose, and then her lips.

"Now, I'm off to Julianne's for a little father/daughter collision. Come to my house tomorrow for dinner at six."

"You think everything will be hunky dory by then?" Her legs wobbled.

"I'm sure of it."

Chapter 19

Angie waved as she drove up Jake's curved, tree-lined driveway.

"Couldn't wait for you to arrive." Jake's towering figure smiled from head to toe in front of his rambling brick and rock ranch-style home decorated with Christmas lights and garland. His face was a whirlpool of fun.

Her heart jumped. "I'm glad you're so happy to see me. Makes me feel loved."

"You are loved...very much." He grinned. "Tillie Mae has dinner ready for us. Come on in."

A lofty Christmas tree twinkled in the foyer.

The formal dining room's chandelier glimmered over an exquisitely set dark wood table. Jake slid a chair out for her. Would this be the evening of love, laughter, and happy planning she hoped for? Had Jake talked to Julianne?

Jake cupped her hand in his and said the blessing.

"Darlin', is there...uh...anything you'd like to

discuss about...our...a...married life together?" Jake arched a brow and offered her some popovers.

"We haven't set a date." She slathered butter on the roll.

"We're about to. Any questions?"

"I've heard that we should discuss money and who does what in the house. Several of my friends have offered me unsolicited advice."

"Okay. You mean like cooking, cleaning, and laundry?"

"I suppose so."

"Tillie Mae can do the first two if you wish. Do you mind doing the laundry? I guess she can do that too."

Did he have some distasteful habits she needed to know about? With that perpetual gleam in his eye that sent her heart reeling, he must be okay. She had her share of inclinations. Should she tell him she ate breakfast bars in bed, sometimes didn't get dressed till noon, and had thirty-six tubes of lipstick, all is varying shades of pink? Naah, she'd surprise him.

"How often does Tillie Mae help out?" Angie finished her roll.

"Now she comes once a week unless I ask her for special occasions like tonight, but she's willing to come more often if we need her."

"Can you afford for her to come more often?"

"Sure, we'll be fine."

"Really? We've never compared notes on finances. I hope you're careful with money." She regretted her comment, but he'd tended to spend freely on dates. However, he did drive a seventeen-year old Ford Taurus. She gulped and prayed. "Do you want to pay the bills?" She sent up an arrow prayer.

"Sure. I've done it since I was sixteen." He sipped some iced tea.

She hated doing that since Ansey died.

"I've managed to put away a few bucks. Don't worry. My children's inheritance is separate and safe too."

No sign Jake was ruffled. The tremor in her stomach eased. And, his good looks teased her heart. Be careful. *Help me, Lord.*

"Do you have ideas for investments?" He stabbed a bite of steak.

"Not really. I trust you." She patted her lips with her napkin.

"I'm assuming we'll live here, and we can sell or rent your house." Jake leaned in, his eyes searching hers.

She swallowed hard. "I suppose I can live here, but don't know what to do with my home. I love it." A wave of melancholy swept over her.

"Sure, we'll wait on this. Still like to travel?" Jake finished his baked potato.

"I'd like to. Just haven't done much. I'd love to see Paris." The thought of France sent sparks into her yearning heart.

"I want you to be able to spend as much time on your design business as you like. I'd just like a little attention sometimes, especially on weekends."

"Sounds fair. You'll have more of my time than that." Her stomach flipped over his sparkling eyes.

"I'd like to ask you something." She pondered her words.

"Shoot."

"You're always so dapper, except for one thing, your muddy boots. Why?"

"Just a joke between Sophie and me. As long as I had muddy shoes, she knew I'd been out with the animals. No horsin' around, so to speak."

"Was there ever a need for her to worry?"

"Never." He looked her straight in the eyes.

"I believe you."

Jake took her hand. "Let's go to the den."

Rumblings seemed to be coming from outside but no sign he noticed. What was happening?

Jake's housekeeper stepped into the room. "Mr. Stewart. Miss Julianne is here to speak to you."

"Please ask her to come in." Jake squeezed Angie's arm.

Angie scooted onto the sofa next to an exquisite nativity, then sprang to a straighter position. Nervousness nailed her to the seat.

"Hi, Dad. Mrs. Cooper." Julianne nodded. "Dad, would you give Mrs. Cooper and me a few minutes alone?"

Jake hesitated. "Of course, honey. No fireworks though, okay?"

Jake whispered to Angie. "I'll be right outside, but don't worry. Her bark is worse that her bite."

"Thanks for the encouragement." Angie locked her hands together.

Julianne smiled, Bible in hand, and glided to the spot next to Angie.

What a beautiful girl with long, lean lines and flowing dark hair. Her warm doe-eyes smiled. "Mrs. Cooper, you probably know that Dad and I had a talk earlier today. I love my father and listen to him."

"Oh, honey, I don't doubt...."

"It's true I didn't want you two to marry."

Angie gulped.

"But that's not why I didn't call you. After Dad told me he had to fly to see Mrs. Leeson, my dearest friend called from Colorado to tell me her fiancé had jilted her. She begged me to come at once. I had every intention of calling you as soon as I arrived there, but one distraction led to another. Breaking away from Emily with her heart in shreds proved impossible."

"Of course." Angie twisted in her seat.

"In my quiet time this morning, the Lord spoke to me in some scripture."

Julianne had sought the Lord so murder mustn't be involved. Angie breathed a little easier.

Julianne opened her Bible brimming with hand-written notes. "In Ephesians 5:1 and 2, I read, 'Imitate God, therefore, in everything you do, because you are His dear children. Live a life of love, following the example of Christ....'"

"Love those verses." Angie let the scripture sink into her soul.

"Mrs. Cooper, I humbly ask for your forgiveness in not making time to talk to you and for not wanting you to marry my dad. I now offer you my love and acceptance. Dad has told me how happy you make him, and that makes me happy."

"Of course I forgive you." Angie reached over and hugged Julianne. Looking back, they should've talked to their children privately sooner. A calming balm flooded her.

Jake appeared at the doorway. "Are two of my favorite girls ready to go outside?" He gripped them in a bear hug and led them to the back door. As they stepped onto the back patio the night lit up with shimmering candles in the hands of their families.

His and hers, big and little ones.

Happiness pulsed through every inch of her.

Somewhere Over the Rainbow began.

All smiling. They formed a semi circle and began singing.

Jake enfolded Angie in his embrace. She melted.

Would her dreams come true? Could this be happening? Were there tears in Jake's eyes too?

He took her hand and knelt by her side. "For God and our beautiful family to hear, my darling Angela Elizabeth Hemphill Cooper, I love you. Will you marry me...next Saturday afternoon at two in the little church by the river in Gunter?"

With her heart leaping out of her chest, Angie mustered, "Yes!"

The crowd burst into clapping and whistling.

"Oh, Grams, wait and get married with Brad and me on Christmas Eve. A double ceremony! We talked about it and really want you too."

Whoops and hollers shrieked through the backyard.

"Thank you both. We appreciate your offer, but I can't wait." Her heart danced, and heat rose in her cheeks.

The glint in Jake's eyes was like the summer sun after a hard winter.

"And, honey, we wouldn't consider intruding on your special day. We're ready now. It's the right time for love!"

Jake hugged her. "And, your daughter Susan and her family will be here Wednesday, in time to help with the festivities. How do you feel about Paris for our honeymoon?"

"Overwhelmed and ecstatic."

In one group thunderous reply the family shouted, "WE LOVE YOU!"

Chapter 20

Angie couldn't have imagined a more perfect December day. Crisp, snowy, but sunny. The small white church adorned in white poinsettias, mistletoe, and jingle bells filled to overflowing with family and closest friends. This tiny house of worship could be called the Church in the Wildwood after the hymn of the same name.

Her choir friend Joan sang her favorite hymn. *Yes, Lord, how great Thou art!*

Angie gazed into the dark eyes of the man she loved, her daughter Susan and her dearest Southern Belle Dixie-Lee by her side as matrons of honor. She repeated her marriage vows, ending with a resounding, "I do."

Jake shouted his "I do!"

He picked her up and swung her, landing her gracefully in front of the preacher. He kissed her like she supposed Rhett Butler had kissed Scarlet. Would he sweep her off to the land of rainbows, via Paris, and then back to good ol' Gunter, Texas, so they could live happily ever after? Pretty good for two sweetheart baby boomers. As dear Hattie Pearl had told her, *love isn't only for the young but for all who are brave enough to embrace it*.

Frank Sinatra's piped voice drifted through the church giving her giant goose bumps.

"Could love really be lovelier? Second chances with both stilettos on the ground? Hardly. She floated in the arms of her new and handsome husband. Who said she couldn't fly?

A graduate of the University of Texas, Lana has been a teacher and long-time volunteer. She was a lay therapist with the Texas Department of Human Resources, a Discussion Leader in Bible Study Fellowship, a Stephen's Minister at her church, and currently plans and facilitates a group called *Simply Social* that encourages women with conversation, friendship, and humor. Please visit her on facebook and on her blog: lanakrusebabyboomers.wordpress.com.

Lana and her husband David are members of Stonebriar Community Church, where Chuck Swindoll is pastor.

They are the parents of two wonderful children and Mimi and Pop-Pop to six brilliant and beautiful grandchildren.

Dear Reader,
I hope you have enjoyed my debut novel It's the Right Time for Love! For more fun, please read the other excellent books in the Collection:

Avoiding the Mistletoe by Anne Greene

The Matchmaking Widow by Linda Baten Johnson

Jingle Belles and Christmas Beaus by James Yarbrough